DEVIANT SOUL

Damaged Devils #2

Charity Parkerson

Punk & Sissy Publications

COPYRIGHT

—Warning: This book is intended for readers over the age of 18. Some of my books contain allusions to past abuse and trauma.

CHARITY PARKERSON

Editor: BZ Hercules & Consultants

CONTENTS

Introduction

HE WAS TRAINED TO kill. In the process, he lost his sanity and his soul. Onyx doesn't see any of that when he looks at Seven.

Seven is one of countless boys who trained through an underground program to follow the worst of orders. He broke free a long time ago. Now he uses his skills on his terms, but his sanity can't be recovered. No one knows him. He's

1

simply a shadow. A nightmare. Except there's this one guy he can't shake.

The way Seven slips in and out of his life drives Onyx crazy. He wants to hate him. Seven is too hard to resist. Just when he thinks he's finally made some headway towards a real relationship, Seven's secrets come crashing down on them. Now Onyx has a choice to make. He can believe the worst or follow his heart. Either way seems equally doomed.

Deviant Soul is the second book in Charity Parkerson's Damaged Devils series. These are dark romance stories with crime lords, assassins, and sociopaths who find their hearts. They are best enjoyed when read in order.

Author Note

THIS IS A DARK romance series filled with possible triggers. If you need a list, you can skip to the content warning after the About the Author page or check my website: charityparkerson.com/damaged-devils

CHAPTER ONE

A TUNE HUMMED THROUGH Seven's head as he skipped through the warehouse. He moved silently with each footfall by bouncing on his toes, exactly as he had been trained to do. It came as naturally as breathing. Nine bodies littered the area. According to his radar sweep, that should be everyone, but he didn't want to get caught off guard. Seven bounced from room to room, checking everything. He didn't make mistakes. Today would be no different.

Satisfied with his work, he returned to the bodies and sent proof of death to check the final box on his contract. It was a good day. The men were pieces of human shit. He had made an easy three million. Seven felt like ice cream. Cold and smooth. Damn. He really wanted some ice cream. Seven skipped out, turning out the lights as he went. He chuckled as he realized what he had done. Silly Seven. The place was set to blow in fifteen minutes. Whatever. Fifteen minutes of electricity saved.

Without looking back, he closed the door as he left. A truck he had bought under the table for five hundred bucks waited nearby. Seven climbed behind the wheel and headed for a motel room he had booked earlier. It was a by-the-hour establishment that only took cash and saw nothing. Seven headed inside and showered. He hurried, since he had gooey chocolate goodness on the brain and still so much stuff to do.

Cleaned of the blood, Seven hit the road again. He headed for a secluded area in the swamp. It was a place he knew well. Seven fit in with the silent killers that slithered and crawled through uninhabitable land. He, too, had survived in places where no human should have been. Seven readied the truck for disposal. He poured acid on the clothes he had worn, since fire would cause smoke. He tossed the dregs back in the truck before pushing the truck into the thick, unforgiving waters. Seven stood watch until the entire vehicle disappeared and the final bubble popped. When the water no longer stirred, he danced away, skipping and twirling. Music played inside his mind, reminding him that beauty existed in the world. Hidden nearby, he found the second truck he had bought, paying cash. Seven climbed inside and headed for a hotel near the airport. Fire trucks screamed past. Seven only heard the music in his head.

At the hotel, Seven parked where he knew no cameras could see and ditched the truck. He had already removed the tags and VIN. It would be days before anyone realized the truck was an abandoned vehicle. Then they would simply have it towed for scrap, since it was attached to nothing. Seven climbed onto the hotel's airport shuttle bus as if he belonged. In minutes, he was at the airport. By hour three, his flight landed in Vegas. He easily got lost in the sea of faces before hitting the food court at the MGM for his much-deserved ice cream. Seven popped one earbud in and listened to this month's favorite song on repeat while he walked the strip and ate. The music detracted from the screaming homeless, and the half-dressed women asking for money to have their picture taken. Vegas was always the same. Still, he had some time to kill before a private flight took him home. Seven also needed to check out of the hotel he had booked for the weekend in Vegas as a cover. He had left a credit card with a five-hundred-dollar limit at the bar a few hours before flying out under an alias.

Someone had picked it up and made charges all over town while he was gone, just as he hoped, giving him an alibi. His rewards points were piling up in Vegas. It was the perfect town to disappear and reappear—like magic. Seven popped into the mall to make a quick purchase before wrapping things up in Vegas. Then it was only a quick hour-and-ten-minute flight to Tijuana.

From there, Seven headed to the place he always went when he made it home from a series of jobs, Black Heart Tattoos. A bell jingled above the door as he stepped inside. Onyx's head turned his way. The music inside Seven's head turned into a love song as a smile exploded across Onyx's face.

"Whoa. It's Seven. I thought you forgot about me. It's been like six months."

Seven skipped across the space between them and held out the rainbow-tailed unicorn he had bought Onyx in Vegas. "Sorry. I bought you this, though."

The sexy way Onyx's dark eyes moved over Seven before focusing on the unicorn made Seven purr inside. He reached for the unicorn. Seven fought the urge to leap over the counter and climb him like a tree. "This is cute. It reminds me of you."

Seven fought a blush as Onyx put the stuffed animal on display on a shelf behind the counter.

Onyx spoke over his shoulder. "You getting more lines tonight?"

"Yes. Twelve, please." Seven recounted in his head every life he had taken in the six months since he last saw Onyx. "Yeah. Twelve."

With a sweeping motion, Onyx directed Seven to the tattoo room. Seven set his backpack aside and peeled off his shirt as he went. Shirtless, he climbed onto the table.

Onyx went to work, cleaning the spot next to all the other tiny lines on his back, tracking his kills like a man marking his cage walls with a rock. Seven needed the reminder. There were more than he wanted, even though none of it mattered. There wasn't a single line on his back for anyone the world would miss. That mattered to Seven. Still, he held himself accountable.

Onyx waited until he etched the first line in Seven's skin before he spoke again. "Are you going to tell me where you've been?"

A smile tugged at Seven's lips. "And lose my mystery? You don't want that."

For a moment, only silence met his words. "Yeah, I do," Onyx said finally. "I worried about you."

Seven lost himself in the pain for a moment, savoring the scratching on his back. It numbed his mind. His loud brain was always there, reminding him he was crazy. Finally, Seven hummed. "Mhmm. Well, first I went to Massachusetts and then to New York. From there, I went to Mexico City for a while before heading to Spain for a wedding. Then I had to work in Vegas." He skipped the swamp, but that was for the best. Onyx thought he was a travel nurse, and that was why he was always gone. Seven didn't want to lie, but it wasn't like he could tell the truth.

"Maybe one of these days, you'll tell me what these lines represent."

"Maybe it's people I've killed. Maybe I'm not a very good nurse."

Onyx chuckled. "Dark." He squirted cold water on Seven's back and then wiped it away before swiping something cool across the fresh lines. Then his mouth touched Seven's shoulder. Seven bowed his head, giving Onyx better access to his nape. Onyx nibbled his skin, making Seven take a slow, deep breath. "What will you do when you run out of skin on your back?"

Seven scrambled to think straight. "I guess you'll have to start on my front."

Onyx's tattooed hands squeezed Seven's side, massaging. "I think you should let me ink something else on your ass."

"Like what?"

"A butterfly," Onyx answered between kisses. "Definitely a bright, beautiful butterfly. Just like you. Fuck, Seven. You make me want to hate you sometimes. Why do you go away and then reappear like nothing happened? I'm stuck, sitting here waiting."

Seven couldn't think straight with Onyx's lips on his skin. "Don't pretend I'm the only one. You're not waiting."

"Would you believe me if I said I am? You're the only one for me."

Seven turned and drew Onyx between his thighs. He didn't answer because Onyx didn't want him. Not really. Onyx knew their moments together and nothing more. He didn't recognize the crazy in Seven. Maybe that was why Seven couldn't stay away. It was that and the way Onyx's brown skin mesmerized him, taking away the ugliness inside his head. Seven lived for the short bursts of having Onyx's hands on him, making him feel like he wasn't a freak.

He slowly dragged Onyx's shirt up and over his head.

Onyx let him have it. "I should lock the door."

"Do that."

In a flash, Onyx's mouth covered his. Seven surrendered to the emotions stirring inside him. The way their tongues played always made him hot as hell. Onyx had a talented mouth, and he liked using it. Being with him was like controlling fire. It felt impossible, yet powerful. Suddenly, Onyx tore himself away and headed for the front room. Seven watched him go. Onyx was all sinewy muscle. Watching his body move made Seven's brain fuzzy. He wanted to run his fingers through Onyx's jet-black hair and ride that perfect body. In a matter of seconds, Onyx returned. He closed the door between the tattoo room and the front, giving them twice the privacy. Then he was back, sucking Seven's tongue.

Seven went to work on Onyx's jeans, setting the man's erection free. When he dove his hand inside Onyx's underwear, Onyx made a sound like he was in heaven and Seven swore it felt like Onyx's accent vibrating around his tongue. Onyx was the only person on the planet who made Seven feel normal. It didn't matter to him if Onyx fucked everyone else when Seven wasn't around, as long as Onyx didn't turn his back on him. Seven was fucked up like that. He needed the time they spent together. Otherwise, he might fade away.

Onyx hadn't been just talking shit. He wanted to hate Seven. Sometimes, he thought he already did. Then Seven would turn up out of nowhere and Onyx was on him like a fly on shit. He didn't think he could be blamed. Onyx had never met another damn soul who matched Seven. He was unique in every possible way. Each time Onyx thought he would give up on Seven, here he was, reminding Onyx of all the reasons he couldn't say no. He wanted to tell Seven to get fucked. Onyx wanted to claim he didn't want this. Instead, he found himself on his back on a tattoo table, condom in place, and Seven on his dick, proving how dumb he really was.

Seven was something else, though. He looked like the devil and tempted him just as hard. His dark green eyes always looked sweet, despite the long scar that ran down his cheek. That mark proved Seven had seen some stuff. He had other scars too that broke Onyx's heart. In fact, a couple on his back looked like bullet wounds. But his body... goddamn. Perfection. Oddly, though, Onyx was fucking fascinated by Seven's mind. He had never cared about that shit before. But Seven could be almost childlike one second and look deadly the next. He drove Onyx wild with curiosity. Seven just made him insane. End of story.

"So beautiful. I've missed you." Onyx tried locking his back teeth so he wouldn't say anything else. Seven felt like heaven on his cock. Desire made him weak. He lasted five seconds before his mouth got the best of him. "Tell me how to make you stay."

Seven kissed him and set a pace that stole Onyx's last brain cell. His asshole was so hot and tight. Fuck. It wasn't fair. Seven held all the cards. Unexpectedly, Seven's mouth moved to Onyx's ear. His motions slowed. It wasn't sex any longer. They made love as Seven whispered against his ear.

"You're my unicorn. There isn't anyone else, but you'll hate me if I stay. I won't be enough for you."

Goddamn, Onyx's chest hurt. They had been doing this shit for six years. Six goddamn years. Honestly, the first few he hadn't taken things seriously. But for the last three and a half years, no one but Seven would do. He couldn't stand for anyone else to touch him. Seven had Onyx tied up in fucking knots for six mother fucking years. The idea that Seven still thought Onyx could want anyone else was so goddamn ridiculous he didn't know where to start. Onyx was angry and turned on, and fucking aggravated as shit. He didn't know what to say or do to convince Seven to stay. Hell, Onyx didn't even know where he went when he disappeared. Frustration welled inside him until he thought he would explode.

Onyx cupped Seven's face and forced him to hold his stare. "Please." He had never begged a single soul for anything in his life. Seven had him on the edge in every way. Onyx didn't even know what he pled for at this point. Maybe just a fucking chance to try.

"I'm not going anywhere. Come for me."

It hit Onyx. His orgasm was the only currency he held. Once he came, Seven would be gone. No matter what he said. Onyx had to get more reassurance. He snagged Seven's waist and held on as he slid off the table. Onyx stood and turned, setting Seven on the table. Disappointment etched Seven's features until Onyx peppered him with kisses. He kissed his way down Seven's body.

"Tell me again you plan to stay."

A ragged-sounding breath escaped Seven. "I do."

Onyx bent and nuzzled Seven's cock. "Not good enough. Tell me you'll come home with me and go to breakfast with me in the morning."

Seven ran his fingers through Onyx's hair. "You don't want that, sweetie. If you really knew me—"

Onyx straightened and moved away to grab his pants. He didn't want to hear excuses. Onyx was done being Seven's plaything, only to be tossed aside once he had his fun.

He made it two steps. "I'll go home with you tonight."

Onyx glanced over his shoulder with his eyebrow raised.

Seven swallowed. "And go to breakfast with you in the morning."

He didn't immediately give in. "Promise me."

While looking pale and ridiculously innocent, Seven nodded. "I promise."

That was good enough for Onyx. Seven had said the words now. Onyx knew himself. If Seven couldn't or wouldn't keep his word, then he would finally be done. Onyx didn't mess with people whose word didn't mean shit. He turned back and immediately went down on Seven. Seven's hips left the table, chasing Onyx's mouth. A cry reverberated from the walls. Onyx licked and sucked. He used every bit of talent he possessed to drive Seven wild. The moment Seven blew, Onyx swallowed the cum filling his mouth and dragged Seven to the edge of the table. He was buried inside Seven's ass to the hilt before Seven stopped shaking. While holding Seven's stare, Onyx thrust, taking what he wanted.

He made sure Seven knew it was him while praying Seven saw how he felt. There was no one else. Seven had ruined him. He was so wild, crazy, and giving. How could anyone else compare? Onyx needed Seven to recognize his feelings and give him a fucking shot. His anger grew again. The sound of skin slapping skin filled the room as Onyx's rage had him taking Seven harder and harder.

Seven stroked his chest. "I promise." The whispered words sounded as loud as a gunshot. They set Onyx free. He blew. A gasp tore from his throat. He tried getting as deep as possible as he filled the condom with cum. Onyx wished it was Seven's ass. He wanted to watch his juices drip from Seven. A wave of sadness washed over Onyx as the final wave of his orgasm passed. It would likely be a long time before he touched Seven again. Seven always broke his heart. He doubted tonight would be any different.

CHAPTER TWO

ONYX LIVED IN A tiny apartment not far from the shop. It was noisy. Seven felt overwhelmed by the competing sounds of cars, music, and yelling. He wanted to put in his earbuds to drown it all out, but he didn't want to make Onyx feel ignored. Seven white-knuckled his backpack instead, trying to hide his anxiety. It was already painfully obvious Onyx was angry with him tonight. He didn't want to make things worse and

Seven got it. It had been six months since his last visit. He didn't usually go so long, but he had been extra careful. It wasn't that Seven hadn't wanted to see Onyx. In fact, it had been hell staying away, but Seven's life was dangerous. He had recently pissed off a powerful crime lord by purposely botching a job. Seven lived by his own rules, and no one owned him. If he didn't feel right carrying out what was asked of him, then he didn't do it. That simple. Unfortunately, Archer Woods didn't see it that way. He had hired Seven to do a job. Archer had expected results. He didn't like the path Seven had chosen. Oh well. A cackle rang out in Seven's mind.

"The place is a bit of a mess. I didn't plan to have company tonight."

Seven's gaze barely skirted the small living room before returning to stare at Onyx. He was the only reason Seven was there. "I lived on the streets as a kid before getting scooped up by the system. You never have to worry I'll judge you."

Onyx took his hand and led him to the couch. They sat close enough their knees touched. "See? That's exactly the type of thing I want to know about you."

"Why?" The question popped out without thought.

Onyx smiled.

Seven fought a sigh. He was so gorgeous.

"What do you mean, why? Because I like you. Damn."

"Oh." Tires screeched outside. A horn blew. Seven rubbed his arm hard enough for the friction to heat and distract him.

Onyx's gaze dropped to the motion. He stood and reached past Seven to click on a sound machine. The sound of the ocean filled the room. Lapping waves had Seven's shoulders relaxing.

"Sorry. I know the place is loud. It's close to work and I can't afford much else."

He wished Onyx would stop apologizing. "It's fine."

Onyx's gaze latched on to where Seven still tried rubbing off his own skin. "Clearly, it isn't."

Seven clasped his hands and shoved them between his knees, trying to force himself to appear normal. "It's fine," he repeated, sounding firm.

Onyx snaked his hand between Seven's clasped hands. He moved slowly, drawing Seven from his inner panic. Their fingers linked. He brought Seven's hand to his lips and kissed his knuckles. Seven forgot to breathe.

"I think it's been long enough for that new ink, if I'm careful. Come shower with me."

Seven was here. He couldn't just sit and rock himself. "Okay."

With Seven's hand in his, Onyx led Seven inside what had to be his bedroom. The bed was unmade. Everything was black. The curtains, sheets, and comforter were all solid black. Onyx kept moving until they stood inside a minuscule bathroom. It was nothing more than a sink, toilet, and walk-in shower. They would be super close under the water. Seven was cool with that.

Onyx kissed him.

Seven lost himself. The love song fired to life inside his head again. He fought the urge to start singing. Onyx worked on stripping him. Seven let it happen. He was always alone and hyper-independent. Handing over control was a thing he reserved for only Onyx. Onyx treated him like a king. He was the only person who felt real to Seven. Humanity had been tortured from him years ago.

"Where's your mind?"

Seven almost giggled at the question. He had lost that thing a long time ago too. Fortunately, he understood Onyx wanted to hear his thoughts. "I was thinking about how you treat me like a king and I fucking hate that work kept me away for so long. Sometimes, I resent it." Always. He always resented it, but he didn't know how to stop.

"I'm always bitter about it, but I know you need to make money."

No. He didn't. Seven had millions stashed all over the world. In fact, he should take better care of Onyx. He should start tonight. "You should hurry so I can wash your back."

Onyx's mouth lifted in one corner. "I think you just like having me naked."

33

"You're so pretty."

The smile that exploded across Onyx's face made Seven warm and fuzzy inside. He made a silent vow to try harder. Onyx deserved better than him, but—for whatever reason—Onyx chose to spend time with him. He didn't want to fail.

Their shower wasn't sexual. It was intimate, and exactly why Onyx wanted it. He took his time washing every inch of Seven. Onyx touched him everywhere. The loving way Seven watched him had Onyx's throat tight. He had dreamed of having Seven here. Onyx needed to give him every reason to stay.

With their bodies clean, Onyx killed the water and then took his time drying Seven's skin. Seven let everything happen to him. So trusting. He was beautiful. Onyx wrapped the towel around Seven's waist and stole the chance to kiss his neck.

"I think I have an extra toothbrush somewhere."

Seven released a ragged-sounding breath. "Mine is in my bag. I came straight from the airport to you."

Damn. The confession hit Onyx in the chest. Seven was impossible to resist. "Good. Let's finish this so I can hold you." Onyx forced himself to pull away and move to the sink. He worked on putting toothpaste on his toothbrush while Seven got his from his bag. Side by side, they brushed their teeth. It felt so personal. Onyx wanted to scream that this was the life he wanted with Seven. He worried Seven would run if he said the words aloud.

With their nightly routines finished, Onyx took Seven's hand and headed for bed. He wished like hell he had cleaned. Now he looked like a slob. That was one more reason for Seven not to come back. It was bad enough the place was loud and small. He didn't look like much of a prize. Onyx turned on the bedroom's sound machine to drown out the traffic while Seven tossed his towel in the hamper. Then he let Seven climb in first so he would be against the wall. Onyx always felt ridiculously protective of Seven. He wanted to be between Seven and the door in case of an intruder.

It was ridiculous. No one would choose his place to rob. Plus, Seven had a very sexy, cut body. He could likely protect himself. It wasn't Seven's looks that had snagged Onyx, though. He possessed an innocence and vulnerability that called to something inside Onyx. Onyx needed to keep him safe. Seven needed a keeper.

Onyx climbed into bed next to Seven and cuddled as closely as he could. Their lips found each other. They lingered. Onyx petted and kissed Seven until they finally drifted. Even in his sleep, he floated on a cloud of happiness. Until a painful kick landed against his shin. Onyx's eyes shot open. Confusion crowded his brain. Seven fought for his life against an invisible foe.

Onyx panicked. He had never seen anyone fight so hard against a dream. A punch hit him in the chest. He tried protecting himself while helping Seven.

"Whoa. Wake up, baby. You're having a nightmare. Wake up!"

At his shout, Seven's eyes flew open. He looked half crazed as he scrambled away and tucked himself into the corner. Onyx never dreamed he could make himself so small. His eyes shot around the room, but Onyx got the feeling he wasn't seeing anything but the visions in his head. He was afraid to touch him or speak. Seven looked terrified.

Onyx's heart broke. He had known. It wasn't like he was stupid. He knew Seven was a little messed up, but Onyx wasn't afraid of that. The wildest creatures were always the most loyal. Onyx settled back down on his side and rubbed the empty spot on the mattress beside him. He closed his eyes so Seven wouldn't feel on display, and he waited. The entire time, he kept up the motion of rubbing and patting the spot where Seven should be. It took some time, but eventually, Seven wormed his way beneath Onyx's hand to steal the pets for himself. Onyx fought a smile. He didn't want Seven to see his satisfaction. They just had to get through this first night. Onyx needed Seven to see he could handle whatever kept Seven moving nonstop. Seven's lips brushed his chin in the sweetest of kisses. This time, when they fell asleep holding each other, nothing disturbed them.

CHAPTER THREE

THE SCENT OF BACON cooking pulled Onyx from his sleep. His eyes opened to find Seven's side of the bed empty. He rolled so fast, he got a twinge in his back. Onyx didn't understand how Seven had gotten past him without waking him. Through the open bedroom door, he spotted Seven dancing. A smile exploded across Onyx's face as he watched Seven twirl around the room. In nothing but his underwear, he looked fucking adorable.

Onyx climbed from the bed and found some shorts. He needed a closer look.

Onyx half expected Seven to stop, embarrassed by getting caught. Instead, when Seven spotted him, he snagged Onyx's hands and kept dancing. He burst into song. Onyx couldn't stop smiling. He had thought Seven had in his earbuds. Instead, it was music inside his head. He lured Seven in close and kissed his ear. Seven kept dancing but slowed things down. He switched to singing a love song. Onyx pressed his lips to Seven's shoulder and fought a smile. Seven had one hell of a singing voice. Onyx hadn't been this happy in years.

"I thought I was taking you to breakfast."

Seven stopped singing, but he didn't stop slow dancing. "You were sleeping so prettily, so I placed a grocery order. I wanted you to wake up smiling."

As if Onyx could be any other way with Seven around. "It smells delicious."

Seven stopped dancing and dragged Onyx to the stove. "I made bacon, sausage, biscuits, and hash browns. Hopefully, you like at least one of those things. Oh." Seven jumped and spun. "I also got you these." He grabbed a bouquet of roses that sat on the counter nearby. Seven held them out with a blush.

Onyx brushed fingers with Seven as he accepted the flowers. His chest felt full. No one had ever bought him flowers. He brought them to his nose and sniffed. "Thank you. These are amazing."

"You're amazing." Seven turned away as he made the claim, as if embarrassed by exposing his heart.

Onyx's cheeks hurt. He had never smiled this much in his life. Onyx set the flowers aside and molded his body against Seven's back. With his arms wrapped around Seven's waist, he kissed Seven's shoulder. For the first time, it felt like the right time. "I need to ask you something."

Seven tensed. "What?"

Onyx fought back a wave of panic. He already knew he would get shot down, but he had to try before Seven disappeared again. "I want a real shot. Obviously, I know your life is crazy, and I don't really have much to offer, but I want to know you're mine and only mine." He hesitated. Onyx hated to beg. "Please, just think about it."

For a moment, Seven didn't speak. He no longer felt stiff in Onyx's hold. Onyx took that as a win. Finally, he felt Seven take a stuttered breath. "I'm a mess."

"I'm unbothered."

"You don't really know me."

"So let me in."

Seven dipped his chin, staring down the line of his body. He took another deep breath. "We'll go to my place after breakfast."

A triumphant smile exploded across Onyx's face. Seven wouldn't regret him. Onyx would make damn sure of that.

Inside, Seven was in full-on panic mode. Onyx wouldn't want him anymore very soon. He would be lying if he said he didn't want more with Onyx. The guy was amazing. He deserved the world. That was exactly why he shouldn't be saddled with someone like Seven. Nonetheless, he dressed and waited for the inevitable as soon as they finished eating. His insides shook. Seven had never brought anyone home. Everything about his place screamed he wasn't a travel nurse or right in the head. Seven didn't want to kill Onyx. He would have no other choice if Onyx exposed him. Seven's stomach heaved at the thought. He couldn't do it.

Seven would have to disappear instead. Fuck. He didn't want to start over again.

"You ready to go?"

Seven faked a smile and nodded. He worried the gesture looked as pained as it felt.

Onyx crossed the room and took Seven's backpack from him. He helped Seven put it on and then brought Seven's hand to his lips. "Don't look so worried. I'm a lot harder to scare than you think."

Seven hoped that was true. He worked up a genuine smile for Onyx. "I'm thrilled at the idea of being exclusive. Don't get me wrong. I'm just scared you won't really like me for me for long. You've only had me in small doses."

A sexy smirk touched Onyx's lips. "Those small doses have ruined me for anyone else. Don't worry, baby. You already have me wrapped around your finger."

They would see. If Seven planned to take a chance on anyone, it would be Onyx. Together, they headed outside. They stopped next to Onyx's Harley.

"I need an address."

Seven really hoped this wasn't a mistake. "I'll guide you there."

"All right." Onyx straddled the bike. He smiled over his shoulder, and Seven's heart skipped a beat. He climbed on behind Onyx with his heart in his throat. Seven wanted to make him happy. No one had ever made him feel the way Onyx did. He took a leap of faith and directed Onyx to an abandoned warehouse district on the edge of the city. If Onyx was confused as Seven sent him zigzagging through the empty streets, he didn't mention it. When they reached their destination, Onyx looked over his shoulder with his eyebrows raised. Rather than explain, Seven climbed from the bike. Onyx followed.

"Where are we going?"

"My place." Seven headed for the door and lifted what looked to be a rusty panel. It was fake. The piece hid the high-tech fingerprint lock beneath. Seven didn't check Onyx's reaction as he unlocked the door. When he heard the high-security locks disengage, Seven pushed open the door and led Onyx inside. The lights flared to life as he stepped inside. "Here we are. Home sweet home."

Onyx turned in a circle.

Seven tried to stand still and not hyperventilate as Onyx eyed his things. He knew how the place must look. It was a warehouse, but he had made it his own. The place had taken him years to perfect. It was one big open space with a kitchen, living room, bedroom, and office. Plus, he had a skating rink and arcade games. Everything he missed as a child, Seven created for himself now. A huge jukebox sat next to a pool table. Seven imagined he looked ridiculous to someone like Onyx.

"Can I get you something to drink?" Seven had to say something, and that sounded like something a normal adult would say.

Onyx finally focused on him. His expression was unreadable. "What are my options?"

Seven glanced toward the kitchen. "Um. Honestly, probably not much since I haven't been home in a while." He twisted his fingers. Seven didn't know what reaction he expected, but he also didn't think the hammer had fallen yet. His nerves frayed. He hated feeling out of control. Seven shifted from one foot to the other. It wouldn't be long before his mind made him do something irrational.

"You don't have to stay if you don't want to be here anymore." The words burst from Seven in his growing panic.

Onyx's expression cleared. He closed the distance between them and helped Seven take off his backpack. "Why wouldn't I want to stay? This place is every bit as unique as you. I love it."

Seven eyed Onyx, trying to decide if he meant it. "Do you want to pull your bike into the garage?" Seven asked the question slowly, waiting for the other shoe to drop.

"This place has a garage too?"

At Onyx's surprise, Seven's shoulders relaxed a hair. Onyx sounded genuinely excited. "Yeah. It's through here." Seven took the backpack from Onyx and set it aside before heading to the left to a metal door. He punched a code in to unlock it before pushing his way inside the garage.

The automatic lights came on as they stepped inside.

"*¡Dios Mio!*"

Seven smiled at Onyx's reaction. "I'll open the bay door for you."

Onyx headed for the nearest car instead. "Is this an Aston Martin Vulcan? I thought there were only twenty-four of these in the entire world." Before Seven could respond, Onyx moved to a different car. "And a Lykan HyperSport. These two cars alone are worth like seven mil." He eyed the rest of the garage. It dawned on Seven he had made a mistake as Onyx turned his way. His expression had closed again. "What do you really do for a living?"

Seven froze. He didn't know how to respond. As good as he was at telling when other people lied, he wasn't a good liar. That was why he didn't see Onyx as often as he liked. Seven didn't want to lie to him.

"Is it drugs?" Onyx asked before Seven could respond. "I know you don't have family money. You said you were homeless as a kid. What are you mixed up in? Is it the cartel?"

"It's not the cartel." Even Seven heard the incredulous edge to his voice.

Onyx's shoulders visibly relaxed. "These cars aren't mine." The lie burst from him and then Seven couldn't stop. "I get a discount on the rent here because the owner keeps some of his things stored here."

The line between Onyx's eyebrows said he was every bit as skeptical as he should be. "Is the owner part of the cartel?"

Seven huffed. "For fuck's sake. No one is in the cartel. He's a prominent plastic surgeon in California. We met when I picked up a job at a hospital there. He owns a practice right outside L.A. with some of the most exclusive clients in the world. He has a house in Baja, and he got this place for his car collection." Seven shrugged. "The rent is cheap." He bit his tongue to make himself stop talking. Desperation already clawed at his chest. Seven couldn't keep lying. He would never keep all this straight. Damn. He felt sick. Seven didn't want to lie to Onyx. Onyx would hate him if he knew the truth. He already looked ready to split.

A hint of panic threatened to turn into a raging anxiety attack. Seven had already been out of his league before Onyx saw this place. Now there was a surgeon out there who obviously cared enough about Seven to rent him this awesome place for cheap. Onyx couldn't compete with that. He had to know more.

"Are you dating this guy?" Onyx didn't know why that was the question that popped from his mouth, but he wanted to punch himself.

Seven looked devastated. "Why would you ask that? I thought I was dating you."

Something deep inside Onyx completely melted at Seven's words. He sounded so heartfelt—like they had always been in a relationship. Onyx felt the need to explain. He motioned toward the cars. "This guy trusts you with all this. He must think a lot of you. That sounds like someone who cares."

Seven shrugged. "I have one of those faces."

A smile exploded across Onyx's face. "You do have a very sexy face. I'd trust it with anything."

Seven didn't look appeased. "You just don't trust me enough to believe I'm not seeing anyone else."

Guilt hit. He realized this was likely why Seven hadn't wanted to let him in. The minute he had, Onyx proved he wasn't worthy. "You're right. It's great you made a friend willing to cut you a deal like this. Times are tough everywhere."

Seven still looked stiff. "He's not my friend. He's just my landlord. I just happened to be in the right place at the right time. He wanted someone to keep this place up and I was in between apartments. Since I travel for work anyhow, it didn't really matter where I lived." Seven made a helpless gesture. "It was just blind luck I ended up in the same town as you."

Onyx moved closer. He wanted to touch Seven. "That sounds like fate to me. So..." Onyx wondered how far he could push things now that Seven finally admitted they were a couple. He snagged Seven's waist. "You know, technically, we've been dating like six years. I'd say we've moved slow as hell. Maybe we should speed things up a little and actually talk about our feelings and shit."

"I kill people for a living. This place and all these cars are really mine."

Onyx kissed Seven, cutting off the nervous spew of nonsense. It was obvious Seven was scared of commitment. Onyx needed to remind him why he had said yes to this. "Stop running," Onyx whispered between kisses. "I want you. I want this." Seven clung to his shoulders as Onyx kissed his way to Seven's ear. "You matter to me. Tell me you care about me too."

"You're the only person I care about."

Onyx grabbed Seven's ass and lifted.

Seven wrapped his legs around Onyx's hips.

Onyx headed back inside Seven's gigantic apartment. "My bike can wait. I need cuddles now." He felt Seven smile against his neck. Onyx knew everything would be fine. He had finally caught the man he had been waiting on forever. Onyx would keep him too busy to get away.

CHAPTER FOUR

AFTER SPENDING THREE NIGHTS at Seven's place, Onyx had to get back to work. He resented every mile between them, but Seven had picked up a shift at a hospital just across the border, so Onyx felt a little better about leaving. That was Onyx's second phase of permanently winning Seven. He hoped to convince Seven to take a full-time job close to home. That was a big ask. Onyx knew it. Seven obviously made gangster bucks working around the U.S. He doubted any hospital or doctor this side of the border could offer Seven his worth. Onyx just kind of hoped he would be worth staying for, even if the money wasn't so great.

"He lives. I wondered if you were ever coming back to work."

Onyx fought an eye roll at Angel's shout as he came through the door. They had worked together for years. Angel was like a brother to him, but he could be nosy and obnoxious. "I never miss work. A few days is nothing."

Angel stepped into his path. His wide chest and huge tattooed arms took up too much space. "Wait. There's something different about you. You seem a little too relaxed. Did you finally give up on that loco dude and get some ass?"

"Don't call Seven that. He's different. That doesn't make him crazy."

Angel winced. "Damn. He's back in town, huh? Wait. He stayed more than one night?"

Onyx bit back a smile. He didn't know why he didn't want to seem too happy, but he wanted to grin like a fool. "I stayed with him."

Angel's eyes widened. He ran his fingers through his dark Mohawk. "You're kidding. What's his place like? I bet it's unicorns everywhere."

A laugh burst from Onyx without his permission.

"Ha," Angel crowed. "I knew it. I bet he lives in Playas or something like that."

"Something like that," Onyx said, keeping things vague.

"Damn, dude. Some people have all the luck. He always smells so good. I'm not surprised he's expensive."

Onyx really wanted to move on from this conversation. "Did I miss anything good while I was gone?"

Angel shrugged. "Nah. That one dude who always tries to get your number stopped by, but I sent him on his way. Your boy might be loco, but that one asks too many questions. He has mean eyes. That's no *bueno*."

As much as Onyx hated to agree with anything Angel said, he had to admit he was right on this one. The guy had started showing up about six months ago, dropping in occasionally. He never got any ink. Just sniffed around, acting the flirt, but he left Onyx cold. "Thanks for that. I haven't figured out how to shake him, but I can't have him fucking up things with Seven." He had just nailed Seven down. Onyx couldn't lose him.

Angel made a hissing sound of disbelief. "So it's like that?"

"You know it is." Onyx had been blindsided by Seven a long time ago, and he still hadn't recovered. He wasn't about to lose the guy when things finally started going his way.

"All right, then. I got you the next time he comes in."

That drew Onyx up short halfway through setting up for his first appointment of the night. "What's that supposed to mean?"

A bright smile lit Angel's face. His whiskey-colored eyes flashed with good humor. "I'll take one for the team. He's low-key kind of hot, in a scary way. I can turn up the charm. He won't know what hit him."

Onyx shook his head, fighting a laugh. "You have fun with that." Onyx couldn't stop smiling. Angel was a mess, but he was loyal. If he said he would keep Onyx's part-time stalker away, then he would. That was one less obstacle in his path. Now, Onyx just needed to get to work.

Having to professionally clean a bloody shower was one of the many reasons Seven hated taking local jobs. There were just too many variables. It was tiresome, and kept Seven away from Onyx longer than he liked tonight. It was a bit ridiculous how quickly he had gotten attached to waking up to Onyx's sexy face. He had one quick errand to run before heading to the tattoo shop. Seven used public transportation so he would have an excuse to ride home with Onyx. He loved being on the back of Onyx's bike. It was fun, clinging to Onyx while the wind whipped over him. Seven liked picturing himself flying.

He got a lot of strange looks on the bus, but Seven always felt like everyone stared at him. Tonight, it was for a good cause. Onyx always worked with Angel on Thursday nights. Seven enjoyed being extra weird with Angel. It was fun to watch him while he tried to decide if Seven was truly nuts. Spoiler alert. He was. Seven fought a laugh as he headed for the door to the shop. Someone held the door open for him as he carried a man-sized teddy bear into the building. He spotted Angel immediately.

"Whoa. What's this? Are you trying to humiliate my boy?"

Seven flashed Angel a huge smile over the top of the bear's head. "What do you mean?"

"You bought him a stuffed bear."

Seven swung the bear over the counter, seating it to face Angel. "Correction. I got him that unicorn on the shelf behind you because he's my unicorn. This bear is for you because you are a sweet, sweet bear."

Angel's expression was priceless. His entire face went through a series of hilarious changes before landing on melting. "Awww. This guy really is cute, my dude. This is nice of you. No one has ever bought me a stuffed bear."

"Well, now you can't say that." His skin tingled. Seven swore he felt the moment Onyx stepped into the room.

Angel's face lit with a huge grin. "Check it out, Onyx. Mine's bigger."

A sexy-sounding chuckle rumbled behind him. Seven took a breath and turned. He swore little hearts appeared around Onyx's head like a cartoon. A happy sigh rang through Seven's mind.

"Dude, hide. Here comes the creeper."

Angel's words barely registered before Onyx snagged his waist and hauled him into the tattoo room. He closed the door behind them.

Seven blinked. "What just happened?"

Onyx looked guilty.

Seven's inner lie detector braced for the worst. He had a bad feeling he was about to hear some bullshit.

Before Onyx got the chance to answer, Seven heard a familiar voice on the other side of the door. His blood froze.

"Is that Onyx's bike outside?"

It couldn't be. Seven had been so careful. How had Archer found him? It hit Seven. He asked about Onyx. Panic struck. He fucking asked about Onyx. Not only had a crime lord tracked him to Tijuana, but he also knew about Onyx.

"He's with a customer. Can I do anything for you? I'm free."

Seven listened to the conversation between Angel and Archer with his heart in his throat. He wasn't scared of Archer. Seven wasn't afraid of anyone. The worst had already been done to him in his life. But he was terrified of what Archer might do to Onyx. Archer could be cruel. Seven had ensured the money had been returned to Archer after he chose not to fulfill their contract. Well, half the money. Seven had done half the job

Archer hired him to do, so he was owed half the fee. He imagined Archer didn't see it that way. Now he was here for Onyx. Seven had to do something.

His gaze shot around the room. There were several things he could use to kill him, but then Onyx would likely freak. Fuck. They had to get out of there. It was the only option.

Seven pressed against Onyx's body and touched his lips to Onyx's ear. "Is there a back way out of here?"

At his whispered question, Onyx looked relieved. He nodded and took Seven's hand. There was a door on the opposite wall that Seven had always thought was a closet. It led into a small kitchen. Seven supposed it was their break room. There was a metal door that led into the alleyway. They stepped out into the warm night air. The moment they were free of the building, Onyx chuckled.

"I feel dumb running from a customer, but that guy is relentless. He keeps showing up, looking through all the artwork, and chatting me up, but he never gets any ink. It's like he's stalking me or something."

It was definitely something. Archer obviously knew Onyx was connected to Seven, but—until now—Archer hadn't known where to find Seven. He had likely followed Onyx home each night, hoping Onyx would lead him to Seven. Now he could. Archer could and would torture that info from Onyx if he had to do so.

Seven tried to play it cool while he had an internal panic attack. "I've got your back. You'd be surprised how good I am at getting away from creepy men."

"That actually doesn't surprise me at all." Onyx backed Seven against the alleyway wall and crowded his space. "Someone as sexy as you probably has men stalking them all over the world. Admit it. I've got a lot of competition."

For a moment, Seven let Onyx distract him. "No. You're so far ahead of everyone else, I can't see anyone but you. There's no comparison."

Onyx touched his lips to Seven's and Seven let the usual love song play out in his mind. They didn't have time for this, but Seven couldn't stop. Their tongues stroked. Seven melted. He couldn't let anything happen to this man. He wouldn't.

Seven pulled back and kissed the corner of Onyx's mouth before dipping beneath his arm. "Just give me a second," he called over his shoulder as he silently skipped down the alley. He bounced on his toes perfectly to hide the noises of his footfalls. Then he peeked around the corner of the building. There was a black SUV on the opposite corner. Onyx's bike was only feet away. Seven quietly made his way to the motorcycle. In a matter of seconds, he had it silently rolling. He pushed it into the alley and out of sight. Onyx's laughter echoed down the alley when he spotted Seven with his Harley.

"Come on," Seven said as he ran past with the bike.

Onyx was hot on his heels.

The backside of the alley led to the next street over. Once they were at the corner, Onyx took over. He climbed on and Seven scurried on behind him. In seconds, they were on their way. Seven didn't know where they were headed. All he knew was he had to save Onyx. Nothing else mattered.

Three nights off from work and one night on and Onyx found himself right back at Seven's place. His life felt on the precipice of something huge. He felt like they were about to take a leap. Onyx hoped whatever came next meant they got to sleep next to each other every night. He had gotten used to soothing away Seven's nightmares. Now he never wanted Seven to face them alone again. Unfortunately, Seven also wouldn't sit still tonight. That had Onyx on a different edge. "Do you want to tell me what's wrong, baby?"

Seven glanced his way. Onyx fought the urge to leap from the couch and physically stop Seven from leaving him. Seven looked ready to run. "I want to ask you something, but I know you'll say no, so my mind is going a million miles a minute trying to decide how to make you say yes."

Onyx blinked at the rapidly paced words that spewed from Seven. He hadn't expected any of them. "Okay. Maybe just ask and let me help you figure out how to convince me."

A sexy smile exploded across Seven's face. He bounced across the room and straddled Onyx's lap. Onyx was pretty certain he would say yes to whatever, with Seven on his lap.

"Run away with me."

For a moment, Onyx's brain glitched. He wasn't sure he heard Seven right. "What?"

"I can afford to support us. Come travel the world with me. I don't want to leave you behind again."

Onyx stared at Seven in silence while the question swam through his mind. He kind of wanted to say yes. In fact, his lease was almost up, and he had been tossing around a crazy idea of doing tattoos at conventions. Running away was actually better than trying to convince Seven to work locally for less money. Onyx had a tattoo artist buddy who traveled from convention to convention, doing tattoos for two or three days only in each town. The guy bragged about how huge the money was since people loved immortalizing their con experiences. He had planted the seed in Onyx's mind. Now the man he wanted more than his next breath offered him the final push he needed to put himself out there.

Seven started to push from Onyx's lap. "Sorry. I knew you'd say no. It's too much to ask."

Onyx snagged Seven's waist so he couldn't get away. "No. I'm just thinking. This is a big move for us. I don't want to take it lightly." He stared at the open hope on Seven's face. If he got cold feet now, he might never get this chance again. Onyx felt himself nod before he knew for sure how he would answer. It was obvious his heart knew. "Yes." His voice got firmer by the second as the decision solidified in his mind. "I want this. In fact, this is kind of perfect. There's a plan I want to run by you about my career. But mostly, I just don't want to be without you again."

"Woot!" Seven covered his mouth as the shout escaped him. His eyes swam with happiness. Onyx couldn't stop smiling. Seven dropped his hand. "I'm so happy."

Onyx was too. He couldn't wait to start this new chapter with Seven. No matter how unexpected. Onyx wanted to be wherever Seven went. Too fast or not, everything felt perfect in his heart.

Chapter Five

THE SPEED THINGS MOVED was exactly as fast as necessary. Not only had Seven not wanted to give Onyx time to think, but they also didn't have time to waste. With Archer on his trail, Seven had to stay a hundred steps ahead. Archer Woods had been smuggling guns, money, drugs, cars, and whatever else was needed to fund certain underground operations into the U.S. for twenty years. He hadn't gotten to the top of a huge criminal organization by being dumb. Archer had somehow linked Onyx to Seven. Seven had to assume Archer had some way to track Onyx. That meant starting Onyx's life over from scratch. Seven had to be smarter than his foe.

"You're spoiling me. It makes me uncomfortable."

Seven tried to look as innocent as possible. "This is all necessary purchases. You need a U.S. phone line and there's no need to pay for a storage unit for your stuff when there's plenty of space for everything at the warehouse." Plus, Seven had anti-tracking devices scrambling the warehouse's location. Nothing within five miles could be picked up clearly on satellite. Every current device on the market made for tracking scrambled once a certain point was breached. Seven had bought every abandoned warehouse in the district under the umbrella of a development company. Nothing could be traced back to him. Now he would ensure Onyx also disappeared.

Onyx looked slightly exasperated. "I know, but damn. You already covered the cost of a temporary artist to take my place so I wouldn't leave Angel in the lurch. Not to mention, you're financing this whole fresh start for us. I'm feeling..." Onyx's hands lifted and fell in a helpless gesture.

Seven made the distance between them disappear. He took the phone from Onyx and tossed it on the hotel bed before wrapping his arms around Onyx's neck. San Diego was only their first stop. They weren't far enough away yet. He needed to stop Onyx from overthinking before the guy bolted. "I'm investing in us. Once you start your new venture, you can help financially too. For now, your part is more of an emotional one. You're trusting me to keep us going. That means everything to me. You're believing in us. That's priceless." Onyx was a romantic at heart. Seven needed him to see this in that light. Despite everything, Seven really didn't want to be forced to kill Archer. He would do so to keep Onyx safe if necessary, but it was a better bet to keep Onyx hidden than starting a war. Plus, it was just bad business to murder a client.

Onyx kissed the tip of Seven's nose and squeezed his ass. "You're right. I know you're right. But you best believe, once

I start raking in the dough from these conventions, I'm drowning you in gifts."

"Deal." Seven's face hurt from smiling.

"Until then." Onyx lifted Seven off his feet. "I can repay you in other ways." He took Seven down on the mattress, narrowly missing the new phone. Onyx shoved it aside as his mouth found Seven's. Seven immediately opened for him, needing Onyx's tongue. Onyx's hands weren't still. He tugged at Seven's clothes. Seven's body stirred at just the thought of going further. His pants were barely open before Onyx slithered down his body. Seven lifted his head so he could watch. Onyx held his stare as he dipped his head and licked the cock he had just freed.

Seven's head dropped to the mattress. He surrendered to Onyx's talented mouth. His eyelids grew heavy as the suction on his dick stole his ability to keep his eyes open. All Seven could do was moan and feel. In his thirty-five years, Seven had seen and done a lot of things. He had endured horrors no one should face. Seven could say with confidence being with Onyx was heaven. He didn't believe in a higher power or life after death. Those false hopes had been stripped from him as a child. But Seven believed in Onyx and the beautiful life they could have together. Seven fully believed he could make all his lies a reality and have forever with Onyx.

Onyx growled around Seven's cock when Seven tugged at his hair. Seven gasped at the sensation. He had to see. Seven

86

lifted his head again and watched Onyx bob on his dick. Onyx had his hand inside his pants, stroking himself as he sucked Seven. It was the sexiest sight Seven had ever seen. The combination of suction on his cock and the hot as hell vision Onyx presented made Seven's balls draw up tight. He couldn't stop pulling Onyx's hair, using him. Seven's hips lifted as he rode Onyx's tongue, fucking his willing mouth. He was half mad with need. Seven whimpered as he reached for the release Onyx's attention promised. A cry tore from his throat as an orgasm ripped through him. He filled Onyx's mouth with cum.

Onyx shot upward and claimed Seven's lips. His own cum filled his mouth. Seven swallowed. His soul was alight with desire. Onyx stroked himself faster as their kiss turned wild. He made sounds around Seven's tongue that had Seven ready to climb inside him. When Onyx cried out, the sound vibrated through their kiss. Onyx painted Seven's shirt with cum. It was beautiful. The gorgeous moment seared itself into Seven's brain, doing its part to destroy the ugliness that lived in Seven's head. Their kiss turned sweet as the madness cooled. Unshed tears burned Seven's eyes. He would be whatever Onyx needed. Seven had reinvented himself before. He could do it again. He would do it again. Onyx deserved the moon and the stars. He deserved a good man. Seven didn't fall into that category, but he could. He would find a way.

Life had changed so goddamn fast, Onyx's head hadn't stopped spinning. Once the decision had been made to leave with Seven, they were gone in practically the next breath. Seven had gone on a shopping spree, buying Onyx everything he needed for a new life. He had even paid all the fees to register Onyx for a dozen upcoming conventions, getting his new venture started. Onyx was blown away. He had gone from thinking Seven would never settle down with him to having a whole new life with Seven in less than a week. Now they were two weeks into their new adventure, and Onyx was already addicted. They had to stay like this forever.

Onyx stripped the cum-covered clothes from Seven's body before peeling off his clothes. Nude, they snuggled beneath the covers, kissing and touching. The happiness welling inside Onyx made him feel like he would burst. He needed Seven. Onyx literally needed this life. He had been slowly losing himself for years. As one of nine children, Onyx had never been special. Being the only gay child in a large, God-fearing family made him less than exceptional. It left him ostracized. He had slowly stopped going to family events at twenty-three. By twenty-five, he hadn't even gone for casual visits. It wasn't until he was twenty-nine that it really hit him that the phone calls had stopped. No one even tried on either side to hang on to a relationship. He was alone. Then that same year, Seven had skated into his job, with the oddest of tattoo requests. He had worn all pink except for his unicorn tail. Onyx's face had hurt from smiling as he watched Seven rollerblade around the front room of the tattoo shop. He talked a million miles a minute, but Onyx had no trouble keeping up with every word. Seven was like sunshine. He brought the light and seared Onyx's soul. No one knew how much Seven meant to Onyx. He was everything. Seven was all he had.

Onyx was fully aware he knew nothing about Seven's past. He could piece together enough. The nightmares and scars told him everything. Onyx didn't need or want Seven to tear open his soul, just to paint him a picture. Onyx only wanted to make every day from now on the best days of Seven's life. He wanted to fill Seven with so many good memories, he forgot the past. Most of all, Onyx wanted to be the family neither of them had. He wanted to build a permanent home with Seven. Tonight, that home felt real.

"Onyx."

Goddamn, the sound of his name in such a needy tone had Onyx's heart skipping a beat. "Yes, baby."

"I just realized I forgot to tell you something important when I asked you to run away with me."

Onyx couldn't stop kissing Seven's neck. It tasted too good. "Mhmm. What's that, baby?"

"I love you."

Onyx's head jerked upward. He had to see Seven's face. Seven looked nervous, and like he expected Onyx to freak.

"That's the why. I forgot to explain why I asked you to come with me. I'm in love with you."

Onyx's throat swelled. "I love you too." His voice came out sounding gravelly. Onyx couldn't help it. He worried he might cry. No one had ever touched him like Seven. They were so fucking beautiful together. Onyx was blinded by the perfection. He held the world.

Onyx slowly lowered his head. He held Seven's stare, soaking up the wonderment in Seven's expression until the very last second. Then their lips met, and Onyx's eyes closed. It was as if they sealed a silent promise with a kiss. This was forever. They weren't acting on a crazy impulse. It was just time. Actually, it was long overdue for them to build this life together. Onyx regretted nothing, except that they hadn't run away sooner. They were meant to be.

CHAPTER SIX

ONYX'S FIRST THREE CONVENTIONS weren't
as big as he hoped, but he had still
made a month's worth of wages each
weekend. Then things built up steam.
People started recognizing his work, and
the money doubled and then tripled. By
his third month of doing conventions
every weekend in a different town, Onyx
consistently made enough money that
Seven didn't need to work. In fact,
Seven was right there with him for

each event. He fit in perfectly with the con crowd. Seven dressed up in elaborate costumes. Everyone loved him and people constantly stopped him, wanting his picture. It was as if they both had found their crowd. Seven could be as eccentric as he wanted. No one judged him. More than that, the nightmares stopped.

Seven skipped next to Onyx, holding his hand. He kept stopping, as if trying to get himself under control, but then he was back to bouncing on his toes. Onyx couldn't stop smiling. He lived for the happiness Seven's existence brought to the world.

"Are you going to tell me where we're going? I'm so excited." Seven bounced as he asked the question as if he might literally burst if Onyx didn't tell him.

They walked Central Park. With the streetlamps lit and the sidewalks empty, the place looked picturesque. Onyx had been looking for the perfect spot, but at Seven's question, he realized it was more about the perfect moment. That felt like now.

Onyx pulled Seven to a stop and turned to take both his hands. He held Seven's stare. "I love you."

A bright smile lit Seven's face. "I love you too."

Onyx dropped Seven's hand and reached into his pocket. With a breath for courage, he dropped to one knee.

Seven gasped.

Onyx held out the ring he had bought while Seven had been out buying new costumes. "I've known since you skated into my life that I couldn't live without you and the happiness you bring to my life. Will you marry me?"

A suppressed squeal grew louder by the second until Seven finally set it free. He danced in place, making Onyx's cheeks hurt from smiling. "Yes. Holy shit. Yes."

Onyx shot to his feet and captured Seven's mouth. They smiled so hard during the kiss, they would pull away to smile some more.

"I love you." Seven's voice cracked on the whispered words. "I love you so much."

Onyx slipped the ring on Seven's finger. The moment felt right. Perfect. He couldn't ask for a more ideal memory. They would always have this gorgeous story to tell. Everything with Seven was so goddamn flawless.

"Put your hands up."

Onyx froze.

"Both of you. Hands in the air where I can see them."

Onyx lifted his hands. Everything turned surreal. Life seemed fake as men screamed for them to get down on the ground and the handcuffs appeared. Badges were flashed and rights were read. All Onyx could do was hold Seven's stare and watch as Seven became someone new. His expression turned wild—like a caged and abused animal being put in chains. Something inside

Onyx broke as he watched the love of his life disappear and turn into something terrifying.

"I don't understand." Those were the only words Onyx knew because he didn't understand. One second, life had been beautiful, and now everything was gone.

The walls were bare except for the two-way mirror in the room. Seven sat alone in a hard wooden chair at a plain wooden table. His heart slowly bled, stealing the life from him. But he had been trained to endure, and he would. No one could break him except Onyx. Fuck. Onyx. He didn't know where they had taken him. His poor angel had looked so confused. They had put them in separate cars and kept them apart. No doubt they grilled him now, recognizing he would be easier to crack. They were likely telling Onyx everything, except Seven didn't know what they had. He hadn't done a job in months. Seven was too good to get caught. He never left evidence behind. This arrest could be for a million things. It didn't matter. He didn't need to prepare. Seven had been raised by demons to become the devil. He had gone from homelessness to an orphanage only to be adopted by a society of men who trained assassins. There was nothing any cop could do to him. Except they could hurt Onyx, and that was unacceptable. Seven had to play this just right. By the time the door opened, Seven knew exactly what to do. He pretended to be innocent and scared.

"Mr. Seven. I'm detective Nic Higgins. Do you have a last name? We couldn't find one that seemed real anyhow." The blond detective tossed a file on the table and sat. "Your fingerprints aren't in the system. In fact, nothing about you is in the system."

"Why would it be? I've never done anything wrong in my life." Seven wanted to give himself a bow for his acting skills. He sounded terrified.

Nic smirked and opened the folder. He pulled out three eight by ten photos and set them in a row on the table in front of Seven. "Are you telling me that's not you?"

They were pictures of Seven walking behind Senator Kenneth Yearly with a bloody sledgehammer over one shoulder. Yearly's hands were raised. It looked like the abduction it was. Fuck. The Yearly job had been sloppy. Seven hadn't been given much time to prepare or clean up afterward. He hadn't been meant to harm Yearly. That hadn't been the job. Seven had changed the rules to help a friend. He hadn't known about whatever camera got the stills.

"I do cosplay every weekend at conventions. That's one of my costumes for horror conventions. I don't understand why that matters."

"You're telling me you don't know that man in front of you?"

Seven didn't answer. He just kept staring at the man's cold blue eyes, looking innocent and scared.

"Let me enlighten you. That is Senator Kenneth Yearly. He's been missing for months. Would you like to guess which night he went missing?"

Seven made a helpless gesture.

"This one. With you. This is the last image of Yearly anywhere and he was with you. Tell us now where the body is and give his wife and son closure. Tell me now and maybe we can cut a deal."

The door opened and a man in a suit that cost as much as some people's homes strolled inside. He held a briefcase and was followed by a man whose face

Seven would never forget. Seven couldn't breathe or look away.

"You are to release my client now, without delay. Here's an order from Judge Davidson. As you can see, Mr. Yearly is very much alive and extremely unhappy to see his lover in distress. This is a huge misunderstanding, but we will take a full apology from you and your team into account, when I file civil suits."

Seven couldn't draw a breath.

Nic shot to his feet. "Senator Yearly. Everyone has been looking for you. I'd very much like to ask you a few questions, starting with where you've been."

The slick-looking lawyer leveled a stern look on Nic. "Any questions you have for Mr. Yearly can be directed to my office.

Right now, you have proof of life and no reason to hold my client."

"Look, I don't know who you are, but it's not that simple. My team has spent several months and countless resources hunting for the senator. Someone has to answer for that."

A cold smile pulled at the corners of the attorney's mouth. "I assure you it is that simple, and if you'll read the letter from Judge Davidson, you'll see that it is indeed a closed matter."

Seven couldn't even blink. His gaze wouldn't waver from Yearly. It couldn't be. Another police officer entered the room and removed Seven's cuffs while Nic still sputtered. Seven was too shocked to form words. He tried to hide his reaction. Seven kept his features blank. He was inches from freedom and couldn't give them any cause to hold him.

The attorney helped Seven to his feet. "Don't worry. I'm Murphy Sullivan, Senator Yearly's personal attorney. He's hired me to represent you. Judge Davidson has ordered your release. You have nothing to worry about. You've done nothing wrong."

"What about Onyx?" While Seven's brain might not work correctly, he still knew he had to help Onyx.

"Your friend was released an hour ago. We'll take you back to your hotel room."

Seven's feet moved, but his gaze still wouldn't budge. He eyed every inch of Kenneth, trying to make his mind understand. When their feet hit the sidewalk outside the station, he came to his senses. He couldn't get in the car with these people. Something wasn't right. A limo appeared, and Seven took a step back.

"I can find my hotel by myself."

A shark-like smile stretched Murphy's lips. "Get in the car, Seven. You have questions and we have demands."

Fuck. It wasn't a request. He didn't have any weapons.

Murphy held out a plastic bag to Seven.

Seven realized it was everything the police had taken from him. His engagement ring was inside. They knew about Onyx. He had to go with them. Seven accepted the bag and climbed inside. The moment everyone was settled, and the car pulled away from the curb, Seven broke.

"I sliced Kenneth Yearly's throat and burned his body. So who in the fuck are you?"

Kenneth's mirror image smirked.

Murphy answered. "He's Senator Kenneth Yearly. That's exactly the truth you'll never waver on from this moment forward."

The car slowed to a stop, and the door opened. Archer climbed inside and they were off again. Seven was trapped. His pulse pounded in his ears.

Archer stared at him with cold eyes. "Hello Seven."

Seven didn't speak.

Archer obviously didn't need any encouragement to keep going. "You've been a naughty boy. Lucky for you, things worked out better than I could've dreamed. After some thought, I realized you were right about the senator. He had a sickness. Crazy can't be controlled. That's something you understand well. It was better to eliminate and replace." He held Seven's stare and spoke slowly, letting Seven know that last bit included him. Everyone knew he was insane. "Also, luckily for you, you can still be useful and now you owe me a favor for saving your ass. Killing a politician isn't easy to escape. You would've been hunted to the ends of the Earth. Now all you have to do is keep up a lie. Your life... and Onyx's, depends on it."

Seven's stomach churned. "What lie?"

"That you're the good senator's lover, of course. He ran away after falling in love with you. The shame of hiding his sexuality from the press and his wife drove him to the bottle and to extremes. But after spending a few months in hiding with you, he checked himself into a treatment center so he could become the good man this country deserves. Now he's back and ready to return to his old life. I'll buy this year's election and you'll stand by every word of this. Murphy will represent you. He's a shark, so I doubt you'll ever be personally questioned. But in the eyes of the world, you are now Senator Yearly's ex-lover, and you recognize now that I can get to you. No matter where you go, I can always get to you. I can certainly get to poor clueless Onyx."

Fuck. He had to do whatever it took to keep Onyx safe and Archer knew it. Seven was trapped.

For much longer than he cared to admit, Onyx sat on the hotel bed with his eyes glued to the TV. Every channel said the same thing. Showed the same images. Seven's face was plastered everywhere. Now he knew where Seven had been those six months. Everything felt like a lie. Seven had only come back to Onyx because his heart was broken. Onyx felt like the biggest of fools. Of course, he wouldn't be the only man completely incapable of resisting Seven. He had brought down a whole senator. Seven had sworn there was no one else. The hurt and rage were real.

For two hours, Onyx waited. He wanted to scream. Onyx needed Seven to tell him more lies. He had been questioned for fucking hours. The things those cops had claimed. Onyx still felt cold. But now he wished Seven had killed the man. That would be easier for Onyx to swallow. The knife in his heart hurt too much. He had to pull it out. Then the live coverage began and there Seven was on the screen, right next to the senator, supporting the man who had driven him back into Onyx's arms. An attorney spoke on their behalf. Onyx listened to every word, incapable of moving. The senator had acted out of love. He couldn't face his constituents or family because of the shame. His entire political career, he had run on the hatred for the LGBTQIA community. He had to disappear to follow his heart. Yearly couldn't bear the shame. Onyx hadn't been ashamed of loving Seven. Why wasn't he enough?

He couldn't listen to any more. Onyx shot to his feet and started packing. He would find a different hotel. If Seven came back, he could keep this one. They were done. Onyx was finished swallowing lies. The betrayal felt so fucking deep. While they hadn't technically been together, in Onyx's heart, they had been. Seven had made him believe they were more. But Onyx was just the guy Seven fell back on when he lost a goddamn senator. Hell, he was probably always the guy Seven ran to between heartbreaks. Onyx meant nothing. Getting dragged into the police station was just another straw on the camel's back. He was lucky to come out unscathed. His new career depended on him being able to travel freely throughout the U.S. He was only here on a visitor's visa. There was nothing stopping them from booting him out of the country. Then what? Onyx's dream would be dead. He was so angry about everything, Onyx didn't know where to start, but he knew he couldn't face Seven. Not yet. Maybe never. As far as Onyx was concerned, Seven could have his senator. It was obvious Onyx didn't matter. Instead of coming back here to explain or anything at all, Seven had gone to a goddamn press conference. Fuck him. Onyx was out. He would take his broken heart and go. Seven's senator was back now. He probably didn't plan to come back to Onyx anyhow. Onyx couldn't wait only to watch him disappear again. So Onyx would be the one who vanished. Two could play this game.

CHAPTER SEVEN

By the time Seven had been set free to return to Onyx, he was gone. Seven wanted to be surprised, but he wasn't. The police had likely said lots of horrible, yet true, things. Now Onyx believed Seven had been with Yearly for six months before coming back to him. Seven knew how it all looked. The faked name Seven had convinced Onyx to use, under the guise of protecting him from possible stalkers, disappeared from the websites of his upcoming conventions. So Seven did the only thing he could. He went home.

Black Heart Tattoos looked exactly the way they left it. It wasn't like they had been gone that long. Somehow, it still felt like forever. Probably because Seven had been happy for the first time in his life. That was over. Seven's nightmares had already returned. His soul knew Onyx was gone for good.

As Seven pushed his way inside the tattoo shop, he braced himself to get thrown back out again. Instead, he found Angel behind the counter, looking every bit as broken as him. Neither of them said a word. Angel circled the counter and Seven walked into his open arms. To his absolute horror and shame, the first tears came. He hadn't cried in years. Decades, actually. Seven had thought that part of him had broken. It seemed not. He cried for what felt like hours. Angel let it happen.

"Do you want to tell me the real story? Because I saw your face during that press conference, and I know nothing that lawyer said is true."

Seven cried harder. He hadn't expected any support, but to hear Angel still believed in him was too much. Life had been exceptionally cruel. Seven knew Angel thought he was a little strange because of the way life had shaped him. Yet Angel comforted him when he should have hated him—the way Onyx did.

"It's a lot. You wouldn't believe me if I told you the truth." Seven no longer cared. He was too tired of life to worry about his freedom.

Angel snorted. "Politicians are involved. Nothing they do surprises me."

A watery chuckle escaped Seven. Even to his ears, it sounded hysterical. "That's not the real senator. The real one is dead. I know because I'm the one who killed him."

For a moment, Angel stared at him, expressionless. Then he seemed to come out of a trance. "Hold that thought. Let me lock up and then you can tell me everything."

Seven nodded and then stood there holding himself. A small part of him wondered if he had come here hoping Angel would hurt him. Physical pain was familiar to him. Losing Onyx was a mental torture he didn't know how to survive.

Angel returned to his side. "Tell me how Archer is involved."

Seven blinked. He was exhausted from the constant nightmares. "How did you know Archer was involved?"

A wry smile touched Angel's lips. "Because I'm not dumb. I know when a dude is trying to play me. He asks too many questions about things he shouldn't know." Angel's shoulders fell. "I'm afraid I let some things slip before my suspicions kicked in."

That explained how Archer had known where to look for him. Not that it mattered now. He had always been doomed to have his actions come back to haunt him. Archer had probably called a tip in to the police just so he could rescue Seven, leaving him in Archer's debt. "Don't blame yourself. Archer is dangerous. You're lucky he chose to play nice to get the answers he wanted. He's not known for his kind heart."

Angel nodded, but he still looked upset. He motioned toward the tattoo room and toward the open break room door. "Let's go talk. I get the feeling we both need someone right now."

Seven nodded and headed toward his fate. He would tell Angel everything. Either Angel would freak, or he wouldn't. Either way, Seven was done with people like Archer. He had already lost the only thing that mattered. Nothing that happened to him from here on meant anything. He was done with life.

The Sahara had moved in and set up shop in Onyx's mouth. His eyes were every bit as dry and gritty. Onyx's stomach rolled every time he thought about food. He had lived off nothing but alcohol since he lost Seven. Onyx didn't even know what day it was. He supposed he might die any day. The blackout curtains in his hotel room suddenly opened. Light burned his swollen eyes. Confusion had him scurrying upright. He had gone to bed alone. Of that, Onyx was positive.

The thought of anyone else touching him made him sicker than the cheap liquor.

Onyx recognized the face standing at the end of his bed, but his mind was slow. "I know you. Right?" He didn't know why those were the words he found. Knowing someone didn't explain why they were in his room.

"It's Archer. Not that names matter. We have a problem, and it's time for you to get off your ass and solve it."

The cobwebs cleared from Onyx's mind a little more by the second. He slowly recognized he should be worried. This man was in his room over a thousand miles away from the tattoo shop where they'd met. "This stalker thing has gotten out of control, man. You need help."

A bright smile exploded across Archer's face. It didn't make him any less scary. "You have no idea. Nonetheless, you're fucking with my plans with this pity party. I need Seven to have a reason to live, or he might do anything. Seven is terrifyingly unpredictable."

"What in the fuck are you talking about?"

Archer pulled a face that screamed he thought Onyx was dumb as hell. "Get up and go get your man."

Even though he was confused and wondered if he should call for help, Onyx kept up his end of the conversation... like a crazy person. Maybe he had finally slipped over the edge. "Seven isn't my man. He's a liar."

"Oh, that hardly scratches the surface of Seven's personality. But none of that changes a thing. It's time to play your part."

Onyx pinched the spot between his eyes where pain raged out of control. "What are you talking about?"

Archer's empty brown eyes stayed focused on Onyx like a snake ready to strike. "You have two choices, Mr. Muñoz. Either you can go home to Seven, or I can kill you both. It's up to you. I'm fine with whichever you decide."

He meant it. Fear finally struck. Archer was crazy. Onyx needed to keep him talking while he figured out how to free himself and get help. "Why do you care about our relationship?"

"I don't. All I care about is my plans for the future. Seven is my only loose string. It would be easier to make him disappear, but then I'd have to find a replacement for him too. One I can control. It's easier having your life hanging over his head."

"Too? What are you talking about?" Onyx had never been more lost in his life.

"We don't have time for this. Suffice to say, right now, Seven is doing everything I tell him to do because he knows I'll kill you if he doesn't. With you refusing to go back to him, he's a loose cannon. So, once again, you can go home and live a happy life with than man you obviously love or I can kill you. Make your choice. You have forty-eight hours."

Part of Onyx wanted to call bullshit. All of him wanted to rage against being ordered to be with a liar. He was enraged and hurt. His heart screamed because—goddamn it—Archer gave him the excuse he needed to do the only thing he wanted: be with Seven.

"Boss. Time's up. Cree says housekeeping is headed to this floor."

Onyx blinked at the sight of the man clad in a dark business suit, who appeared from nowhere. It was the senator who claimed Seven had been his lover. His cold blue gaze moved Onyx's way and slid down his body before immediately dismissing him. He had called Archer his boss. Archer had said he had replaced someone to control them. The police had sworn Seven had killed the senator. Pieces clicked together in Onyx's mind. Holy shit. Seven was being blackmailed by this guy with Onyx's life. He had threatened to kill Seven if he didn't go along with this crazy-town plan. Onyx couldn't breathe. He had left Seven for something he hadn't done. They had obviously just gotten dragged into something beyond their control.

Onyx scrambled from the bed. He forgot he was nude until the two men openly eyed him. Onyx couldn't worry about them. He grabbed the nearest clothes and pulled them on. Seven was out there somewhere thinking Onyx had abandoned him at his lowest. Technically, he had. Goddamn it. He felt like the biggest piece of shit. Onyx had been so fucking confused when the police had come for them. After hours of questioning, it never occurred to him Seven might be every bit as clueless. He was such an idiot. Onyx needed to find Seven and beg for his forgiveness. He rushed into the bathroom and gathered his things. By the time he emerged, he was alone. First, he would win back Seven. Then they would find a way out of this craziness together. After that, he was marrying Seven before he got away again. Onyx knew now he couldn't live without his wacky other half. Without Seven, nothing mattered. He had to make this right.

CHAPTER EIGHT

SEVEN KEPT HIMSELF BUSY coloring while Angel worked. Angel had bought him a huge box of various art supplies and lots of coloring books. It was oddly soothing. Seven's mind was never empty, but sometimes he forgot to cry when they were together. Angel never seemed annoyed to have Seven underfoot. He couldn't explain how he had gone from spending years alone to being incapable of sitting by himself. But for whatever reason, the silence was too loud now.

On the floor behind the counter, Seven sat on the lap of the giant bear he had bought Angel and colored the big bubble words in his adult coloring book that read "Fuck everything." That was how he felt these days. He wore a one piece zip-up pair of dinosaur pajamas with zero fucks. Seven's heart hurt. He didn't care about anything. Seven would take any ounce of comfort he could get. It had been three weeks since he set eyes on Onyx. Each day that passed, Seven fought to keep his hurt from turning to anger. He knew he was bad and in the wrong, but Onyx had turned his back on him so easily. Seven couldn't imagine a single thing Onyx could do to make him walk away. He had been prepared to take on the entire world at Onyx's side. It seemed the same couldn't be said for Onyx. His love for Seven had strings. That realization cut.

The bell above the door jingled, alerting the shop of a customer. Seven burrowed deeper into his warm pajamas, trying to make himself smaller. He didn't want to be seen.

"What the hell, Angel? Are you dating someone with kids? What's with all the coloring sheets on the walls?"

Seven froze. His heart clenched. Part of him wanted to spring to his feet and sprint into Onyx's arms. The rest of him wanted to run and hide. His gaze collided with Angel's stare. They had a perfect line of view of each other from where Angel worked on tattooing a customer. Angel's expression matched Seven's shock.

Then Onyx was there. With his back to Seven, he dipped his head inside the tattoo room. "Surprise."

Seven couldn't look away from Onyx's sexy shoulders. He couldn't breathe. Seven had to get out of there.

"Hey, man. I thought you were traveling the world, living your dream."

Onyx moved farther into the room with Angel. Seven stole his chance. He crawled on all fours around the counter, moving silently.

"I was, but... have you caught the American news lately?"

Seven made it past the door of the room Onyx occupied. He shot to his feet and tiptoed toward the front door.

"Wait."

Seven froze.

"Is that Seven's signature on the bottom of that coloring sheet?"

Fuck. Why had he let Angel hang those pages like a proud parent? Why had he signed them like an idiot?

"Hmm?"

Seven used Angel's moment of playing dumb to dart toward the door. His hand touched the door's handle. He pulled slowly, trying to keep the bells from making a sound.

"Stop. Don't take another step."

Seven's eyelids dropped. He drew a slow breath. For a moment, Seven focused on the air entering and leaving his lungs. Then he opened the door and walked away without looking back. His heart couldn't take facing Onyx. He darted down the alley, heading for the back. It was easier to snag a cab there. The shop's alleyway door opened, and Onyx stepped into his path. Their gazes locked. Seven's body went cold as the blood drained from his face. He felt lightheaded.

"Hey, baby."

Hyperventilating looked to be a real possibility. Seven couldn't respond. Every fiber of his being wanted to run.

Onyx took a step toward him.

Seven took a step back.

Hurt flashed in Onyx's gorgeous dark eyes. "I know you hate me now. Hell, I hate me. I shouldn't have abandoned you the way I did."

The love was still there. He was the only person Seven loved. It was so strong and pure. The truth hit Seven. He hurt and always would, but Onyx was right to leave him. Onyx was safer that way. There had been a part of Seven that had been relieved Onyx was gone. That way, Onyx was safe from him.

"I need to get a cab."

The pain in Onyx's expression deepened. "Will you at least talk to me first?"

Seven wanted to stare at him all day, but that wasn't fair. He was poisonous to

Onyx's life. "You made the right choice. Now stick to it and stay away from me." Seven turned away and headed back the way he came. He could catch the bus this way.

"Archer says he'll kill us both if we can't work things out."

Seven froze. Ice ran through his veins. He stared at nothing as rage washed over him. The madness took hold. He became the person who terrified even him. Seven looked over his shoulder, letting Onyx see the man he should fear. "Not if I kill him first."

Seven walked away, leaving his heart behind. It was time for him to break out the mask and go for a hunt. Archer needed to die. That day was long overdue.

Onyx watched Seven go with his heart in his throat. He wanted to run after him and demand Seven listen to him. Seven looked like a stranger. He was hard and cold. The way he threatened Archer had been terrifying. Onyx never dreamed Seven could look as evil as he had in that moment.

The door opened next to him. Angel motioned him inside. "Come on. My customer is gone. I locked up behind him. We should talk."

Onyx had never heard Angel sound so serious. His gaze moved between Angel and where Seven had disappeared. He knew where he was now. It would be better if they talked at home.

"I'm serious, Onyx. You need to hear what I have to say."

Angel's dark tone got his feet moving. He stepped inside. Angel locked the door behind him.

"You should sit."

Damn. Onyx didn't like the way things sounded. First, Seven became someone he didn't know. Now Angel. His life had become a real nightmare lately. He sat.

Angel didn't. He crossed and uncrossed his arms, as if he didn't know what to do with himself.

Onyx decided to help him along. "Seven came to you."

To his surprise, Angel's face hardened. "Well, where else would you have him go? He doesn't have anyone else, does he? You sure as fuck proved he couldn't depend on you."

Angel's fury shocked him, but Onyx knew he deserved it. He had thought it would come from Seven, though. "Things took a weird turn."

Angel deflated. "I know." He rubbed the back of his neck. "Look, I don't know where to start, and I feel like I'm breaking Seven's confidence. It's just I feel like there's a lot you don't know, and you should, but then again, you kind of already proved you can't be trusted with the big stuff."

Onyx tried following Angel's rambling. He understood enough to know Angel knew things he should know. Onyx needed to hear whatever it was. He was finished with being in the dark. "I recognize I made a huge mistake. It won't happen again. These past few weeks have been hell. If you know anything that'll help me, you have to tell me. I love Seven. He's it for me. I can't lose him."

"That senator is a fake." Angel said the words so fast. Onyx might not have followed if he hadn't already surmised as much for himself.

"I know."

Angel didn't look relieved at the confession. "Do you know why he's a fake?"

The leading way Angel asked had Onyx answering slowly, in case Angel wanted to jump in with a better explanation. "I'm assuming it's so that fucking Archer guy can control him for whatever reason."

Disappointment etched Angel's features. "Damn." The quiet curse sounded more for himself than Onyx. Angel swiped a hand across his face and then moved to fill the chair across from Onyx. The tiny dining room table in the break room seemed even smaller with Angel's huge frame sitting there. "You really don't know." Again, the words sounded more for himself.

"Just tell me. Whatever it is, I need to understand." And they were wasting time. Onyx needed to go after Seven.

Angel gave him a sharp nod. "Okay, but I have to start at the beginning, and you have to swear you won't freak or tell anyone."

"You have my word."

"I'll hold you to it. A man isn't shit if he can't keep a promise."

Onyx nodded. They had been raised to solidly believe in men keeping their word. Whatever he learned, no matter how terrible, Onyx wouldn't repeat it.

Angel took a ragged-sounding breath. "Seven lived in the streets as a kid. From his first memories, he was homeless. He doesn't even know who his parents are or why he lived in the streets. That's just all he can remember."

"Damn."

Angel winced. "It gets a lot worse, so hang in there. He ended up in an orphanage where he lived for two years until these men showed up and basically bought him and some of the other boys from the home. They thought they were going to live in a big house with nice things. That's what the men promised. Then they were tossed into cages."

Chill bumps rose on Onyx's skin. He couldn't blink or breathe. The way Seven looked as he had been handcuffed came back to haunt Onyx. He wanted to run to Seven and comfort him. Unfortunately, Angel wasn't done.

"They were made to fight for every scrap of food. The boys literally ripped each other to shreds until only the strongest survived by forming rabid packs. Then those boys were trained to kill more efficiently. The abuse Seven endured."

Angel shook his head. His eyes looked dead, as if he saw something even worse than Onyx pictured. "I can't believe Seven survived. If it were me, I would've stepped in front of a bus a long time ago."

Onyx hated to ask, but he needed to understand. "What was the purpose of all this? Were these people just twisted fucks or what?"

Angel's chest expanded on a deep breath. "The purpose was to make them into elite assassins. To make them soulless killers they could sell to the highest bidder."

Onyx's throat swelled as he recalled the way Seven had looked as he threatened to kill Archer. That was what he had seen in Seven: a murderer.

"Fast forward to many years later," Angel said, continuing as if he wasn't stomping Onyx's heart. "Archer hired Seven to do a job for him. It turns out, surprising no one, Senator Yearly was a sick fuck. He had kidnapped these two guys, hoping to exchange them for the stepson that had escaped his years of abuse. Apparently, Yearly wasn't done with him or claimed to be in love with him or whatever. The stepson lived with Archer, you see. So Archer wanted Seven to free the guys Kenneth had abducted and then negotiate with the senator for the return of the son. He would give Kenneth back the stepson only as long as the senator stayed in Archer's pocket. Basically, Archer would own him. Except Archer didn't know Seven had befriended the stepson. When he set eyes on Yearly, he saw the same sickness in him as the men who tortured him as a child. Seven couldn't go through with it." Angel's chest expanded again.

Onyx was leaned Angel's way, hanging on every word. He thought he would burst. "So what did he do?"

Angel held his stare, as if he expected Onyx would run now. "He returned half of Archer's money and killed the senator."

Onyx's spine gave out. His back melted against the chair. So much flew through his mind at once. It raced in every direction. Seven had told him. He had said everything in that warehouse was his and he killed people for money. Onyx had thought it was nervousness talking, but Seven had told him the truth. Onyx just hadn't listened. The police had shown him pictures of Seven with Yearly. He had been carrying a bloodied sledgehammer. Each breath came harder than the last as realization after revelation landed. All the lines he had tatted on Seven's back. Holy shit. Seven had told him the truth about those as well. The biggest truth of all hit. He was in love with a psychopath.

Chapter Nine

Killing Archer Woods wouldn't be easy. Seven needed a plan. He had time. This was something that couldn't be rushed. He didn't know enough about Archer's security these days. He had stopped sneaking onto Archer's property over a month before their falling out. Seven needed new reconnaissance. He had to keep his mind busy with anything but thoughts of Onyx. Seven had spent his life being the freak. It hadn't mattered before now. He had found some happiness in the small things. Seven loved to dance, sing, skate, and a dozen other things that proved he was free. He had killed the men who had tortured him as a child and bathed in their blood. Seven still smiled at the memory. He felt zero shame. Seven had never cared what anyone thought about his actions. He had survived. Seven did what he needed to do. Onyx wasn't like him. They should have never been.

Seven stared at the ceiling above his bed. A projection lamp next to his bed sent lights and images spinning through the dark. He let the blurry pictures hypnotize him. His mind felt too busy tonight. He needed soothing. A red light that didn't belong flashed in the corner of his vision. Seven's gaze shot that way. Someone had set off the silent alarm. Seven shot to his feet. He tiptoed through the warehouse, listening for any sounds. As quietly as possible, he slid open the hidden wall next to his couch, revealing the tools of his trade. Seven grabbed the white and black mask he wore to hunt. The silicone piece was like a second skin as it molded to his face. The hollow eyes and black stitches across his lips worked like psychological warfare. He wanted whoever saw him to fear for their life. Seven planned to take it.

With a knife in one hand, he slipped into the shadows, staying close to the wall. He needed something solid at his back to keep him from a surprise attack. The metal door between the garage and kitchen opened. Seven froze and waited. A man-sized figure slipped into the darkened warehouse. Seven lunged, overtaking him. Quicker than the intruder could take a breath, Seven held the knife to his throat.

"Who sent you?"

"Um. Me."

Seven immediately dropped the knife from Onyx's throat at the sound of his voice. He was slower to release him. His body didn't like relinquishing its hold. When he took a step back, Onyx spun. He knew what Onyx saw in the dark. The pale face of death. Most people didn't live to tell about it.

For a moment, Seven stood still and let Onyx see the real him. Then he peeled off the mask and moved to return it. He felt Onyx follow. Seven replaced the mask and knife before sliding the wall back into place.

"I didn't want to believe it was true." Onyx's words were slurred. "How can I be in love with someone who kills people?"

He was obviously drunk, which should have made him less appealing. Seven still couldn't make himself look at Onyx. "They were all bad people, if it makes you feel better."

"How bad? Like incurable shoplifting bad or serial killer bad?"

Seven headed back to bed. He still needed the dancing lights. As he settled onto his back, he answered, "If you need to talk yourself into being okay with me, then you're not okay with me."

Onyx sat on the edge of the bed. "That's the thing. I think I am okay with you. No matter the answer. What does that say about me? I mean, you could kill me in my sleep."

"No. I couldn't." Seven took a breath because the instant rage stole his ability to breathe properly. "If you think that, then you never loved me. How could you even say that?"

"I'm just really confused right now." Onyx sounded sad.

Seven rolled, turning his back on him. He wouldn't watch Onyx leave. He heard Onyx take a shaky breath.

"My parents named me Onyx because I was born with black hair and eyes, and they had so many kids, they were running out of names. How did you end up with the name Seven? I feel like I should've asked that before now."

Seven didn't like talking about the past, but he had kind of enjoyed hearing that tidbit about Onyx. "I didn't have a name when I got sent to the orphanage. Everyone on the street just called me Kid. I was assigned to room number seven. So that's what they called me. It stuck."

"Didn't you want a real name?"

Seven shrugged. "What constitutes a real name?"

"I don't know." Onyx still sounded so hurt and sad. It tugged at Seven's heartstrings, but he had feelings too. Maybe no one had ever cared about them, but they existed.

"The thing is, I love you."

Seven rolled at the confession. He needed to see Onyx's face.

Onyx didn't stop there. "From the first moment I met you, you've wowed me. I love your eccentric ways and how you make me smile so hard my face hurts. We were perfect... Weren't we?"

A lump grew in Seven's throat. "I want to say yes, but you think I could slit your throat in your sleep, so maybe not."

Onyx released a tired-sounding growl. "You lied to me, baby. How am I supposed to feel? I'm being serious. Tell me how to feel because I don't know. I believed every word you said when you told me all that shit about being a travel nurse and a doctor renting this place to you, and you were only pretending."

"I tried to tell you the truth."

Onyx's shoulders fell. "I know."

"But you're right," Seven admitted. "I should've tried harder, and I shouldn't have accepted your marriage proposal without you knowing the truth. Honestly, I just thought I could be who you thought I was and then it wouldn't matter who I'd been. Since we started working on your dreams, I haven't taken a single job. I've been right at your side the whole time and I'd planned to never work again. Honestly, I just wanted to be with you and never look back. It was unrealistic. I know, especially with Archer out there, wanting my head."

Onyx scooted closer. "If that's who you want to be, then be that person. I can give you an amazing life. Just let it go and be my husband. Don't look back. Forget Archer and all the rest. Have a normal life with me."

"Archer threatened you. He has to go."

"No. He doesn't. Don't you see? It'll never stop if you don't quit. So you kill Archer? Then what? Someone else steps up to take charge and they come after you next. When does it end? It doesn't until you walk away with me. I'm asking you to do this for me. Just be my husband and let it go."

Seven wanted that. Onyx would never understand how much he craved the beautiful life they shared. He missed the conventions and elaborate costumes.

Seven ached for the life they had built away from the blood and pain. He wanted to be held again while he slept, being kept safe from the nightmares. But he also had to be realistic.

"Archer feels like I owe him now. What if he expects something else from me? You'll hate me if I'm forced to do what it takes to keep us safe."

"I don't think it's possible for me to hate you. But we can cross that bridge when or if we get to it. We'll figure it out together." Onyx took Seven's hand and toyed with his fingers.

Seven stared at the way Onyx stroked his skin. Onyx wasn't asking for much. Yet he asked for everything. Seven could easily do what Onyx wanted, but then again, he would always know Archer was an ax over their heads.

Onyx trailed his fingers from the center of Seven's palm to his wrist. "Let it go." He whispered the words as he made his way to the bend of Seven's arm. "Just be with me."

There was nothing Seven wanted more. He just didn't know how.

The terror of seeing Seven in that mask and the weapons hidden just out of sight still choked Onyx. Apparently, he was dumb or completely insane, because nothing made him stop wanting Seven.

None of those parts of Seven felt real. Seven was the angel in dinosaur pjs coloring at the tattoo shop. He was the man who danced and sang with zero shame, no matter where they were. A million people could tell him in a billion ways how Seven murdered people in cold blood and the image in his head never changed. Seven was his baby. Onyx still wanted him forever. Unfortunately, Seven still hadn't agreed. Onyx didn't know how to convince him. So he kept lightly stroking Seven's skin while silently hoping for the best.

Seven yawned. His eyelids dropped. "Could you hold me? I can't sleep for the nightmares again."

That broke Onyx's heart. He didn't hesitate. "Of course, baby." He crawled into bed and gathered Seven in his arms. The moment he held him, Onyx knew beyond any doubt Seven couldn't lose him. He was a sad, desperate man because he loved Seven more than he loved himself. His lips automatically found Seven's temple and then his cheek. The alcohol swimming in his blood had him floating and ready for more. His heart needed to hold his other half. Onyx's lips kept finding Seven's skin. Seven let it happen. His breathing deepened, and Onyx tried to stay still. Seven obviously needed sleep more than he needed Onyx pawing at him.

The moment Onyx forced his lips away, Seven took his hand and dragged it down his body until Onyx shaped Seven's erection through his pajama pants. Onyx closed his eyes and drew a steadying breath. His fingers found their way inside Seven's underwear. He stroked the soft skin of Seven's hard cock. Seven took a ragged-sounding breath. Onyx's dick tried pushing its way out of his jeans. He kept his touch light, still unsure if he tried to put Seven to sleep or lure him into fucking him.

Seven tilted his chin toward Onyx, openly begging for kisses. Onyx's mouth covered his, and he moved without thinking. He straddled Seven's body. Their tongues played as Onyx tugged at Seven's pants, freeing his erection.

"Please make love to me." The whispered plea between kisses nearly hobbled Onyx. Never in his life had he wanted anyone as much as he did Seven. The ache never eased. It didn't matter if

Seven was a deviant soul, or the sweetest person ever born. Onyx craved every version of him. Part of him wondered what Seven would have been like if he had gotten to be a normal child. At the end of the day, Onyx preferred the uniqueness that was Seven. He was perfect as is.

Onyx molded against Seven, letting the friction of their bodies do the work as their cocks came together. He needed to feel Seven's bare erection between them, rubbing against his. Onyx wanted Seven's cum on his skin. He had the rest of his life to get inside Seven again. For now, he just needed the slow burn of his dick stroking Seven's cock. They felt amazing together.

He explored Seven's mouth, savoring every stroke of tongue on tongue. His body moved without thought, rocking against Seven. Seven gasped, moaned, and held on, driving Onyx crazy with lust. Onyx's head spun with a mixture of alcohol and pure need. The love, though. That outweighed everything. He had to tell him.

Onyx pulled away and buried his face against Seven's neck. "I love you, *mi corazón*. Fuck. I wasn't good without you. I didn't want to wake up anymore."

Seven cupped Onyx's face and forced him to hold his stare. "Don't say that to me. I love you. This is forever. But if anything should happen to me, you have to keep going. I can't live with any other outcome. This world isn't beautiful without you."

"I love you." Onyx had to say it again. He couldn't stop.

"I love you too." Seven pushed, urging Onyx onto his back. Then he worked on completely divesting Onyx of his clothes before stripping. Once they were nude, Seven worshipped Onyx's body. There was no other way to describe the kisses and caresses Seven lavished upon him. Onyx writhed while Seven toyed with his cock, balls, and asshole. He licked a line down Onyx's torso before sucking his dick. Onyx's back bowed as Seven went all in. Seven had Onyx's legs in the air, quivering as he found Onyx's asshole with his tongue and drove him insane. His fingers followed. Using nothing but spit, he fingered Onyx, massaging his prostate while he sucked Onyx's balls. Onyx scratched at the sheets with his mind a mess. Sounds burst from him that would have humiliated him under any other circumstances.

"Fuck me. Please? I want you inside me." Onyx rarely bottomed, but he wasn't opposed. Tonight was one of those nights that he needed the connection. He craved the stretching and the feeling of fullness. Onyx wanted to leak Seven's cum. Neither of them would ever be with anyone else again. Of that, he was sure. They had gotten tested when they first started dating and everything had been negative. Onyx knew in his heart neither of them could stand to touch anyone else. It was them against the world. That was who they were.

Seven didn't question a thing. Onyx knew they were on the same level.

Sometimes, it was like they could read each other's mind. In seconds, Seven had his cock lubed and pressing against the tight ring of muscles surrounding Onyx's asshole. It was the sweetest relief when Seven pushed his way inside. Onyx drew a steadying breath. He felt every inch invading him. When he thought he couldn't take any more, Seven thrust, going hilt deep.

Onyx drew a deep breath. Seven gave him that much before he took Onyx. It was a straight-up conquest. Seven pounded Onyx's ass. The sound of skin slapping skin filled Onyx's ears. Onyx moaned and saw stars. Every thrust hit just the right spot. Onyx couldn't think straight. His mouth didn't care if his mind worked.

"Fuck. Yes. Take it. I want to still feel you tomorrow. Goddamn. You're so big. Shit. I don't want this to end. Let me bust this first one and then I want you to ride my face. God, it's been so long since I ate that ass. Damn. I want to make you come so many times you don't have a drop of jizz left."

"Damn, Onyx. Your dirty mouth is going to make me blow before I'm ready. You're already too tight. I swear you're breaking my dick. You'll be disappointed if you don't hurry."

"Fuck that. You could never disappoint me."

"Then fucking come." Seven accentuated each word with a hard thrust.

Onyx was already too close. He reached down, grabbed his dick, and tugged. He came so hard, he couldn't breathe. His body shook.

Seven made a sound like he was being strangled. His thrusts shallowed. Onyx swore he felt Seven's dick twitch inside him with the power of his orgasm. His body collapsed on top of Onyx's, squishing the mess of cum between them. Their lips met. The moment was perfect. Their fingers linked and realization struck so hard, Onyx tore his mouth away to focus on their joined hands. Seven still wore his engagement ring.

Tears blurred Onyx's vision. "You're still wearing the ring."

Seven kissed the shell of his ear. "Of course. I'm always yours. Even if you never see me again, there'll never be anyone else. I belong to you."

Onyx's throat swelled. The stress of the past few weeks, along with the alcohol and orgasm, combined to destroy him. A tear rolled from the corner of his eye. It slid back into his hair as he turned his face back to Seven, seeking kisses. Onyx belonged to him too. Come whatever may, they were one. He would never let them be apart again.

CHAPTER TEN

Seven skipped down the sidewalk, holding Onyx's hand. He was happy today and well rested, which was an annoying combination for everyone around him. Onyx never lost patience with him, though. He always smiled like he adored this side of Seven. That was good, since he was stuck with Seven for life.

They'd had a good day together, preparing to leave town again. This time,

Seven hooked Onyx up with all the paperwork he needed to live anywhere in the world. It was nice not having to hide. It was doubly nice, Onyx let him freely be himself... minus the killing, of course. Otherwise, Onyx didn't seem to care about any of the other illegal shit. That was good. Not only did it make their lives easier for Onyx to carry all the same faked paperwork as Seven, Seven didn't technically exist in any system. It would be damn hard for him to live his life completely above board at this point.

Soon they would be back to traveling, and Onyx would get back to his dream job. Seven could return to dressing up in costumes and being a big kid. It was the quiet life they both needed. They still had one thing left to do before they left town. Seven was torn on this part. He had gotten really close to Angel. Seven didn't want to say goodbye. They would see each other again. Seven would make sure of it, but it wouldn't be every day like it had been the past few weeks. Seven would miss him.

The bell jingled as they came through the door at Black Heart Tattoos. Angel stuck his head out of one of the room doors and smiled. "Hey, Seven. It's been a few days. I was getting worried."

"What? I don't even warrant a greeting any longer? We've only worked together forever." The laughter lacing Onyx's voice let Seven know he wasn't really offended.

Angel stepped out and pulled the door closed behind him. He raced toward Seven and playfully shoved Onyx aside before wrapping Seven in a bear hug. "Have you come to tell me you've finally fallen madly in love with me?"

Seven laughed at Angel's ridiculousness. "I'm not your type, and we both know it."

Angel pulled away, smiling. "You're probably right. You're too nice for me."

Something unnamed swelled in Seven's chest. Angel thought he was nice. He wasn't used to people having kind thoughts about him.

"We actually stopped by to ask a favor."

Angel glanced between them at Onyx's confession. "Anything. You know that."

Onyx took an audible breath. "I want you as my best man."

For a moment, Angel looked confused, as if the request didn't fully sink in. Then a huge grin exploded across his face. "You're damn right. I'd be honored. More than that, I'd be pissed if you asked anyone else. Just let me know when."

The way Onyx smiled—like he was proud to marry Seven—warmed Seven's chest. "You bet. It'll be in California, just fyi."

Angel's smile never dimmed. "No problem."

Seven twisted his fingers. Nervousness set in. "Also, since you'll be there for Onyx anyway, would you walk me down the aisle?"

Angel's expression went from happy to shocked in an instant. He pulled Seven in for another hug. "I'll do it, but just know

I'm not actually giving you away. That's a deal breaker. I don't want to lose you."

The backs of Seven's eyes burned. He had never had anyone he considered family. Seven had people he visited occasionally. Men who had survived the same hell with him—like his friend Journey. Seven especially adored Journey's husband, Chad. But Angel was different. Seven loved him. He felt real. Few people felt real to him.

Seven cleared his throat, trying to control his emotions. "We'll send you the details. It'll be soon, but we want to find the perfect spot first."

Angel nodded. They held each other's stare. Before he could stop himself, Seven hugged Angel again. Angel was the first person Seven had confided in, and that meant something. It meant everything. Seven had never trusted anyone with his secrets the way he had Angel, and Angel hadn't let him down. There was no way Angel could know how important he had become to Seven.

"I love you, loco boy."

A tear rolled down Seven's cheek at the words. "I love you too, bear." Seven swiped at his face. Onyx held his stare, wearing the sweetest of smiles. Seven knew his life had turned a page. He felt it happen. They would be happy now and forever. Seven felt that deep in his shredded soul.

Black Heart Tattoos' doors had opened for the first time fifteen years ago. Angel had been twenty-five at the time and scared shitless he would fail. He had borrowed money from his uncle to open the shop. Angel had known the money hadn't been gained legally and Rico would break his kneecaps if he didn't repay. He was now debt free. Unfortunately, that didn't mean much.

The time he had spent focusing his everything on making his shop a success had meant any type of personal life had gone out the window. He had blinked and turned forty. The last few weeks of having Seven underfoot had jolted something awake inside him. He was lonely. Honestly, he had known that for a while, but having Seven around doubled the feeling now that he wouldn't be coming around as much anymore.

Being asked to walk Seven down the aisle made him long for something he would likely never have. He had lost his chance to find anyone who would love him. He watched Onyx walk out the door with Seven, staring as they walked down the street together to where Onyx had parked his bike. A sad smile tugged at the corners of his mouth as he watched Seven bounce on his toes and spin. Onyx never let go of his hand. He stayed completely indulgent of Seven's every whim. They were beautiful together.

"You did good, sexy."

Angel's eyes fell closed. His throat swelled. That was the biggest reason no one would ever love him. Angel belonged to Archer and it would always be that way.

CHAPTER ELEVEN

ONYX WASN'T THE LEAST bit surprised that
not a single member of his family had
come to his wedding. Angel had shown.
That was all that mattered. So too
had some guy named Journey and his
husband Chad. Seven had been hazy
on the details about how he knew
the pair. Since Journey looked like a
guy who would kill someone without
blinking, Onyx figured he was better
off not knowing. Chad, on the other

183

hand, owned the biggest porn production company in the U.S. He turned out to be fascinating. Onyx enjoyed watching him interact with Seven. Seven was like a kid, seeing his best friend after years of being apart. He dragged Chad onto the dance floor of the hotel bar and danced erratically around him. The way Chad smiled said a lot. He cared about Seven. That meant everything to Onyx.

"It was a nice ceremony."

Onyx nodded, acknowledging the small talk Journey tried dredging up on his behalf. It had been beautiful. A small chapel right on the beach. Gorgeous. Still, he felt moved to keep up his end. "Where were you two married?" Onyx asked, nodding Chad's way.

Journey's cold gray eyes stayed locked on Chad as he answered. "With our bare feet in the sand in Maracas. Seven was one of the few people there. People like us keep our circles small, but loyal."

Journey's words hit home harder than Onyx expected. He was right. Onyx was one of them. It didn't matter only three people had been there to stand at their backs while they married on the beach. It had been beautiful, and Onyx knew those three people cared more for them than a hundred family members who couldn't be bothered. He would take quality over quantity any day.

The music slowed. Onyx and Journey immediately set their drinks aside so they could join their husbands on the dance floor. He loved the sound of that. His husband. Onyx's dream man finally belonged to him. Angel had found a partner amongst the crowd. Onyx knew he didn't have to worry about entertaining anyone. He was free to enjoy the moment. Their first dance as a married couple. This was his version of heaven.

Seven pressed his lips to Onyx's cheek as he walked into Onyx's arms. Onyx's heart swelled with pride. Soon, he would take his gorgeous husband to bed. They would start the rest of their lives together. He knew Archer was still out there somewhere and could slip back into their lives at any time. But Seven and Onyx had a secret. This was the last night anyone would see them for a long while. Seven knew how to completely disappear. This time, he would take Onyx with him.

No one other than Angel knew about Onyx working the conventions. Seven had set up a way for Onyx to continue to do so under a shadow company name. They would slip into the world of traveling shows, staying hidden in plain sight. Onyx believed in Seven's ability to make it happen. No one paid attention to convention goers. Their eyes slid past people dressed in elaborate costumes—like they were embarrassed on the person's behalf. It was the perfect hiding place.

Truthfully, none of that mattered. Onyx had Seven. He would go anywhere. Give up anything. Their bodies swayed to the music. Seven's breath fanned against his throat. Onyx held the world in his arms. He would never let go.

Onyx carried him over the threshold. Seven knew he stared at Onyx with stars in his eyes. His husband. Seven's eyes stung every time he thought about it. He had a family. A real family. He belonged to someone. It felt amazing. No one could possibly understand. He had gone his entire life alone, surviving the worst with zero comfort. Now he was someone's husband.

"Are you okay?"

Seven blinked, coming back to himself at Onyx's question. He tugged at Onyx's tie, slowly undressing his man. "Yeah. I was just thinking about how I have a family now. I never have before."

Onyx kissed him. It was a sweet whisking of lips. So gentle. "You're damn right. I've got you now."

"I love you." Even to Seven's ears, he sounded on the verge of tears. "I have a last name. A real one." His voice quivered, forcing him to bite his bottom lip. It was funny. He had spent his entire life thinking a name meant nothing. It was just another way to find him. Now he had a genuine last name that he shared with someone he loved. It felt like everything.

"Mr. Muñoz."

Seven shivered at being called that. "Yes, other Mr. Muñoz?"

Onyx smiled. "You're the love of my life."

A love song played through Seven's head. Seven cupped Onyx's dick through his pants. "Then give me what I want."

"Just tell me how you want it and it's yours."

"I want it forever."

A bright smile lit Onyx's features. He loosened his belt and unbuttoned his pants. "That's good since that's exactly how long you're stuck with me, husband."

Seven crawled on to the bed and flashed a wicked smile over his shoulder. "Give it to me."

Onyx laughed. It was a sexy, devilish sound. "There's my little deviant." He set one knee on the bed. "That ass is mine."

Seven tumbled onto his back and waited. He knew soon enough his soul would be set ablaze. It was twice as delicious because it was real and permanent. They had been tested and found unbreakable. Everything was perfect skies from this point. They had each other. That meant they had everything.

Keep an eye out for the next Damaged Devils, *Villainous*.

Please consider leaving a review at the retailer where you purchased this book. Reviews really help with a book's visibility, which allows me to continue writing more stories. Thank you, Charity.

Content

CONTENT WARNING: DAMAGED DEVILS is a dark romance series that deals with dark subjects. There is murder, sexual assault, abuse, kidnapping, and power dynamic relationships. These are anti-hero books. They won't be for everyone.

About the Author

CHARITY PARKERSON IS AN award-winning and multi-published author with several companies. Born with no filter from her brain to her mouth, she decided to take this odd quirk and insert it in her characters. One of her greatest loves is writing morally gray characters. You'll find them scattered throughout her hundreds of titles.

*Eight-time Readers' Favorite Award Winner

CHARITY PARKERSON

*2015 Passionate Plume Award Finalist

*2013 Reviewers' Choice Award Winner

*2012 ARRA Finalist for Favorite Paranormal Romance

*Five-time winner of The Mistress of the Darkpath

Connect with her online:

*Sign up for her newsletter: https://sendfox.com/charityparkerson

*Join her readers' group on Facebook: http://bit.ly/CharitysTribe

* Website : https://www.charityparkerson.com

*A list of her social media accounts and giveaways all in one place: http://hy.page/charityparkerson